Although anxiety provoking for some, Stafford's sensitively written, non-judgemental style ultimately makes TURNED ON a story of hope.

Patricia Mills, Integrative therapist

TURNED ON shines a light on the underbelly and trauma pornography creates.

Jon F., former pornography addict

I've dealt with my shame and guilt about my own actions but this book allowed me to empathize with the women I've used.

Phillip M., former cybersexual addict

If I'd been able to read this book before we went into couples therapy, I'm sure my partner's real-life activities would have been less shocking to deal with.

Gemma S., partner of extreme pornography user

TURNED ON

Intimacy in a pornized society

D. E. Stafford

THE WiTTING PRESS, Cambridge
A WiTTING Original

TURNED ON: Intimacy in a pornized society

First published in 2010 by THE WiTTING PRESS

EDITED AND PRODUCED BY Sandra Stafford at THE WiTTING PRESS,
Cambridge, 2010
PROOFREAD BY Lynn Brown
TYPESET AND DESIGNED BY Paul Barrett Book Production www.pbbp.co.uk
PRINTED BY Labute, Cambridge www.labute.co.uk

British Library Cataloguing in Publication Data
A catalogue record for this book is available from the British Library

ISBN 978-0-9564987-1-7

acknowledgements

My deepest gratitude goes to Martin Young and Tim Ellis, as well as the Monday and Thursday groups who have helped me in many different ways during the process of writing this book. My gratitude also to R, L and H. Let me thank my dear friend Kathy Denny for reading the manuscript in a single day and enjoying it, and Martin Hodges who was there when this book was the tiny germ of an idea in 1996 and who read the final text some thirteen years later.

My special thanks go to Pat Mills for her thoughtful engagement with this challenging text and for her professional support. Also, to Chris Kell for her deep clinical understanding of this book's material and for putting me on the right path for a second time in my life.

Finally a heartfelt thanks to Sandra Stafford – not just for more than two decades of trusting belief in her husband but now for being my editor and publisher.

Author note

The information that provides the skeleton for the story in this book comes from numerous sources that include academic, personal and professional research methods. It must be stressed that this book is a work of fiction but any client-derived information has been consensually given before being heavily disguised.

Real names of pornographic websites, chatrooms and most performers have not been used, since it is not my intent to promulgate such people, products or facilities in this book. The exceptions to this are *Fiesta*, *Escort* and *Mayfair* magazines, which I feel are already likely to be known to many people in the general population of the UK – even those who have little or no knowledge of erotic/pornographic materials.

TURNED ON

The following names of films, performers, film directors and book titles/authors have *not* been changed: Bettie Page (pin-up and fetish model, 1923–2008), *The Notorious Bettie Page* (film, 2005, directed by Mary Harron), *Lilya 4-Ever* (film, 2002, directed by Lukas Moodysson), *Story of O* (erotic novel, 1954, written by Pauline Réage).

contents

prologue

This book is not primarily concerned with judging pornography and cybersexual activities or those who use them. However, it does, through a fictional narrative style, engage with the deleterious effects that high levels of use of such material can have on people – its subtle creep into the social fabric of daily life.

Although *Turned On* is largely the fictional tale of an unconventional 'couple' – Marc and Louise – this man and woman represent a large population of real people encapsulated for many different reasons in a pornized society.

There is no wish to titillate or arouse sexual desire through the material contained in this book. However, the text does deal in the real detail of pornography and cybersexual 'addictions'. *Turned On* is written for both a professional and a general readership. It is not a sanitized, bland, intellectualized or academic piece of writing.

While reading this book, for a short period of time you will be able to inhabit something of the internal mindset of three people: Marc, the highly educated professional man who is a heavy user of pornography, telephone sexlines and related activities; his therapist, who facilitates the unfolding of Marc's personal social history and the process of recovery; and Louise, the bright but lifetime disadvantaged telephone sexline worker whose life will illuminate some of the wider effects of a pornized society.

Marc and Louise's actions and fantasies are not only or always those of troubled people; the roots of their difficulties also lie in the desire, passion and sexual stimulation many, if not all, humans crave in life. However, in our increasingly desensitized, perhaps even pornized, twenty-first-century society, this story may still shock, disgust or even anaesthetize you. Please, look after yourself as you read the story in these pages but know that if a word, phrase or idea shocks you it can be skipped over, moved past, forgotten, *or* thought about, felt, pondered or discussed with someone else. You do not have to enter the 'world' Marc and Louise live in for yourself; this work has been done for you so that you can truly know what it is like.

Turned On is a journey, and within all journeys there are good and bad times. I simply ask that until you reach the end and know the full story – Marc's past, Louise's experiences – you will not judge those involved. When you have read their story, I hope that you might wonder what you can do to initiate positive change for yourself or someone else. I trust that you will understand more about your own position in what is one of contemporary society's most troubling issues.

D. E. Stafford

PART ONE

1 the keys to the sweet shop

29 June 2007

SUBJECT: INITIAL THERAPY SLOT
marc@_____
TO: therapy@_____

Hi,

I recently found your website on the Internet and wonder if you can help me.

For as long as I can remember I have been compulsive about looking at pornography. In the last few years this has manifested itself as an online 'addiction', and also from my use of chatrooms and telephone chatlines I am having what I can now only describe as an affair.

I have never been to therapy before but I have read your website and feel that your experience with difficulties like mine and the way you practise sounds like it would suit me very well.

I wonder if you currently have any of your initial session slots available?

Thanks for your help.

Marc Moreau

When I open the door for the first time to meet Marc, I am instantly aware that he is a handsome man. His green eyes shine under a full head of well-groomed hair, just greying at the temples. He is impeccably dressed in a navy blue suit with white shirt and deep red silk tie. He has something of a 'film star' aura.

'I'm not always this smart,' Marc says, 'it's just I'm on to a meeting after we finish.' He smiles. I smile back. We shake hands and walk to my consulting room, which overlooks a terraced area of my garden.

Marc settles himself into a chair opposite the French windows and smiles at me once more. Despite his well-groomed appearance, I can sense he is edgy and tense. After my usual 'housekeeping' comments about confidentiality and making it clear that this is a 'no obligation' initial session, we settle to work. I begin by saying, 'It's strange to come and talk to a perfect stranger about some of our most intimate thoughts, actions and feelings, so don't feel you have to perform to me. Take some time and let's just feel our way into what you are bringing.'

'Thanks,' Marc says. 'You've obviously done this before!' He laughs. 'No, seriously, you're making this easy for me. I wasn't quite certain what I'd say when I got here. It's one thing writing about what I do – what I'm into with sex – in an email but it's quite different being here in person. You know, I've just sat in my car for the last ten minutes thinking, "I'll drive off now and phone and say I'm ill."'

Marc goes on to tell me about his sexually compulsive behaviours and how these have manifested themselves since he was a child – from looking at printed pornography to watching VHS tapes, DVDs and streaming video, to his addiction to telephone chatlines and, currently, the Internet. But the thing most worrying to him is that he has recently fallen 'deeply, passionately in love with a woman'. The woman, Louise, is a telephone sex worker. She is not of his class, not of his intellect, but is embedded inside his head and his heart.

'Before we had broadband, a wireless router and laptops at home, I think I could handle most things I was into.'

'Most things?' I echo.

'Well, I used to buy magazines … that was okay, although when they stopped censoring things as much a few years back I did go through a period when I was buying mags all the time.'

'Do you know why?' I ask him.

'It was amazing that top-shelf mags were suddenly full of all the sex I previously had to go to the sex shop to get. Cliché that it sounds, I was like a kid in a sweet shop who suddenly had £100 to spend on sweets!' He laughs, and I laugh in response.

Although it is very important to set out the ethical and professional boundaries right from the beginning of the work with someone, I think it is also incredibly important in an initial session to help someone feel at ease and in doing so allow that person to know they are not only meeting a professional but also a human being. Although Marc's sense of humour is being employed in defence of a number of his feelings in the room, I know an initial session is rarely the place to challenge. Engaging with Marc's lighter side allows the two of us to begin to form an alliance and prompts Marc to begin to talk about his sexual predilections.

'Were there other ways you felt out of control with erotic or pornographic material?' I ask Marc.

He thinks for a moment: 'Well, as I said, I think the magazines got out of hand and before I could control the amount I was spending and looking at them, the Internet went broadband. Now it wasn't £100 I had to spend in the sweet shop, it was more like I had the keys to the shop!'

'Suddenly you found there were sweet shops everywhere and there was no need to pay for the sweets?' I reflect and add.

'Mmmm, suddenly there are sweet shops everywhere and they are always full of sweets – no matter how many times you go. They always have your favourite sweets and they give them to you for nothing it seems.'

'And what happens when there is access to all these sweets all the time?' I ask.

'Ha! Good question … You get … fat! Your teeth fall out, you get diabetes and … if you keep going … it probably kills you.'

There is no laugh or smile. For the first time in the session, silence takes over the room. In that silence I begin to pick up on the dark and fearful interior that I am accustomed to meeting in men who bring into the space difficulties with pornography and cybersexual issues. It allows me to tune in a little to what this man needs to discharge.

After a long pause I say to Marc, 'It seems to me that there is anything but enjoyment, anything but pleasure in this "porno sweet shop". Do you know what feeling it *does* give you?' It is a tentatively voiced question. My intuition guides me. It tells me *don't push; Marc is fragile.* His perfect exterior is at deep odds with who he is on the inside.

'There is an awful pain, I don't … I don't know what to do with … oh fuck!' Marc puts his hand across his eyes.

Silence …

'It's okay … you don't have to do anything, you don't have to say anything you don't want to in this space.'

Marc's shoulders are heaving up and down. In front of me is a forty-one year-old man, handsome, beautiful even. To the world he looks like he has everything and yet here he is crying like an infant, remorseful, distraught.

He begins his next sentence through sobs and tears. 'A couple of weeks ago … oh, God … oh, fuck … four weeks ago I saw … My life is a fucking mess … I've made my life … the most awful fucking mess …'

There are times to let people stay and be with their feelings, whatever they are. I am moved by the depth of the emotions Marc is clearly so lost in. To be honest, to see a man cry like this is never easy, even for a therapist, someone who experiences it as part of working life. There is always something that pulls me back to the social normative behaviour about masculinity that I, like so many others, have been indoctrinated with – the idea that 'big boys don't cry' is, it appears, almost impossible to eradicate completely. Nevertheless, I let the atmosphere created by Marc's despair guide me, and in the busy yet silent and motionless space I have to operate from, I imagine what it might be that Marc is so fearful of. His despair is such that experience tells me he will either have strayed into or wilfully navigated to one of a small list of things.

Recovering himself a little, Marc begins to raise his head. 'I really don't know how to begin to talk about this …'

I am preparing myself for what I might hear. Never knowing what might be said in the room, I check in my own head that I have stated everything I feel I might have needed to about harm-to-self and others, about confidentiality. I steel myself for certain subject areas that come up time and again in this particular type of work with men – and sometimes women. I prepare to protect myself from vicarious pornographic trauma.

'… I saw a video that hurt me so deeply, it has shaken my belief and trust in myself. It's confused me and upset me and put me out of balance in a way nothing else ever did and it seems to have made me act in a very strange way …'

Is he talking about pornography as a trigger for some action he has undertaken? Could he have raped someone?

The latter seems unlikely; there is now conflicting evidence of the once-popular myth that pornography use encourages sexual crime.

Has he seen something that has triggered a pre-standing traumatic experience, perhaps child abuse? An act of cruelty? God! It's 12.40 already; I did tell him an initial session can run longer than fifty minutes, but I'd rather keep us fairly tight if I can. I wish he had said more about his parents earlier on in the session. There certainly seemed something odd in that personal social history; mother has some question marks over her … Father? Was he actually ever there in the family? Academics … so often in their own world.

12.41, initial session, I don't want him to unpack too much more, especially if he decides not to do the work. But I don't want to hurry him on, can't hurry him on. Can I stop him? Bloody unconscious; an odd thing. What was it Freud said about the timeless unconscious again?

'I've seen the whole lot I used to think …' Suddenly Marc is brave.

There's not going to be any management I can offer now. I saw him look at the clock; he is going for broke, I can feel it – a door-handler.

'… I really like porn I thought – like my own internal hobby. Don't get me wrong, I'm talking about sex, not abuse – nothing like that. But I've seen all the sexual stuff …'

Here it comes: the test. It's very late, dangerous this late in a session. He's a risk-taker.

'… Almost nothing has grossed me out although I can't say there is anything sexual for me about a Roman shower but felching still gets me off.'

I can see the way Marc looks at me. He wants to know if I know what he is talking about, if I'm up to the job. If I can go with this, then I might be able to help him with his distress.

'Emetophilia,' I say to Marc, 'is often linked with erotic play for people who like to humiliate or be humiliated. There is a link to the idea of spasm, ejaculation and relief for some people. Do you like to watch the felching in a homosexual or heterosexual enactment?'

Did I go too far? Was that too much of a script? Did I sound arrogant? Were we playing for superiority? I take it he knows that emetophilia is a Roman shower – I've never found anyone who admits to being turned on by people vomiting on each other, but that stuff's out there. Licking semen out of a partner's anus, however, does seem more popular!

'Four weeks ago I ended up, by accident, watching a video, some faceless Eastern European girl getting fucked up the arse; they roughed her up a bit. I don't suppose I thought that much of it at first. But by the end … fuck, the end of that video …'

Again I centre myself; I prepare to protect myself however I need to.

'The video made it seem like she was a kid … there was a school photograph … she looked exactly the same in the photo as the rest of the video. I hardly noticed it, I was busy jacking myself.' There is a slightly shameful look on his face. 'But fuck! She might have been a real kid, not some twenty-something pretending; it looked too real for me, there was no "tell" that this was an act. What do I sound like? A paedophile, pathetic.'

'Marc, you are an intelligent man clearly, and yet I hear you say, what was it? "some faceless Eastern European girl getting fucked up the arse". This sounds at odds with how you were speaking earlier in the session and whatever age this female was, I think there is something you are trying to tell me about your feelings. Let's remember the sweet shop analogy from earlier.' I refrain from mentioning that strictly speaking he would be an ephebophile (someone interested in adolescents) rather than a paedophile (someone interested in prepubescent boys or girls). 'I'm concerned where we find ourselves; the time we have left is very short and there is an awful lot to deal with here. At the beginning of the session we said this was an initial session. Do you get a feeling that you'd like this to be more than a one-off?'

·•· ·•· ·•·

In the end, we run over by only a small percentage. Marc fills out the paperwork and we agree to meet for four further sessions to see if therapy really is the right way, in his mind, to deal with his difficulties.

As he leaves the session he shakes my hand again. He adds confirmation that he has found something in the space by placing his free hand gently on the back of mine. I refrain from returning the gesture but, in my mind, I am saying: *I know Marc; I know how you feel.*

2 a life of porn

9 February 2007

Since humankind first began representing the world through pictorial and sculptural means, the human body and its sexual organs have been a prime 'object'. However, the beautifully round Venus of Willendorf with her swollen belly, wide set thighs and large breasts, the Cerne Abbas Giant with his erect penis beaming out from the cut-turf Dorset landscape, and the Shelah-na-Gig medieval Irish fertility figure with her held-open vulva each offer very different reasons for representing adult sexual organs to the world at large than the Internet does for Marc as he searches for pornographic images.

While we might always have to speculate the exact reasons why Palaeolithic figurines of women emphasize and distort the breasts, hips and the stomach, we might reasonably conclude that the people who produced them were involved in at least some form of creative action and communication in producing the artefacts. It may not have been for an erotic purpose; conceivably it may not even have been for the aesthetic pleasure of it either. But it was not a passive act. The creators were fully involved in this process and perhaps its outcome.

Marc's case is quite different …

Marc currently finds himself lost in a twenty-first-century sexual desensitization. Although the last decade has been the most damaging to him as a user of pornography, its grip on him has continually increased over a period of more than thirty years. His involvement in an erotic world is nothing like that of a Palaeolithic man; he creates nothing in the sense of art or communication that someone else might value.

Marc is a user – a passive, zoned-out addict. He views erotica, softcore and hardcore pornography many times a day. As we meet him he is involved in an ongoing telephone chatline affair, although recently it has become a more personal, one-to-one arrangement with the 'operator', Louise, and has ventured into the realms of a private Internet sexroom, and soon they will meet in person for the first time. Marc and Louise are both desensitized – by their past lives, and by a society that accepts sexual feelings as entertainment and employment. There are many similarities that stick the two of them together; you will learn more about this later. At the moment, though, Marc is sitting at a desk in his office writing a financial report about his company. He is thinking about getting himself a coffee – black, strong, no sugar – when he is overtaken by an extremely familiar urge. He re-reads what he has just written: '… and in this case there will have to be cuts.' The word 'cunts' replaces 'cuts'. That's how Marc's brain has started to work: he sees and makes sexual associations around him at all times.

'Cunt' stays with him for a few seconds before he conjures up some mental images. He sees in his mind's eye a shaven vagina. Dark hair is trimmed around the labia, and the 'landing strip' – so popular in the contemporary erotica and pornography he views many times a day – is fully in view. Motionless for some time, he pictures some deep pink labia lips being pulled apart and the sticky wetness of the woman being in full view. He flicks up his Internet browser again and types 'galleries + "wet cunts"' into it. It's 9.56am and he is accessing adult material for the second time that day. The first time he logged in was at 6.14am, when he went straight to his favourite online 'pornhub' and masturbated to a video of two silicone-enhanced blonde MILFs (Mother(s) I'd Like to Fuck). It took him almost twenty minutes to orgasm, and then it was a feeble affair. It always takes him a long time to ejaculate these days. His eyes scan the first page:

<u>Young beautiful girls show their</u> **wet cunts** – *That's no good …* <u>Softcore-black pussy</u> – *Softcore; not at this time of the day, please! …* <u>Teen porn images</u> (<u>Warning: this is a free teen site</u>) … *Blah, blah, blah; God, why must general searches always be teens. We are not all fucking pervs …* <u>Eighteen special 18</u> – *No …* <u>Fluffy wee</u> **cunt** – *Fluffy! …*

<u>Teen</u> – *No …*

<u>Teen</u> – *No …*
<u>Teen</u> – *No …*
Cunt <u>master vagina finder!</u> … <u>Young **cunts**</u> … <u>Lesbian **cunts**</u> … <u>Asian **cunts**</u> …

The truth is that Marc has almost lost interest in searching the Internet for pornography. He now plays games with himself and the search engines, like: *Find a 'watersport' clip in less than ten clicks without using the words 'piss', 'pee', 'peeing', 'watersports' or 'golden showers'.* It keeps him interested in the search process but of course he cheats: he does not stop if he fails to meet his target within his game rules, and he notices the way he lies to himself – even when only *he* sets those rules.

Marc could close his browser right now and get that coffee. He thinks about logging in to a chatroom site where he has an 'Island' set up with Louise. But she is working and he hates just leaving a long ramble to her in their private room. It makes him feel sad and alone. He is unfulfilled if she is not on there live with him.

Marc's first meeting of the day is not until 11am. It's currently 10.12am. He decides to add just one more term to see if it turns up something to interest him. *If the Internet can't find what I want … After all*, he thinks to himself, *I had forgotten to exclude teen sites from my original search anyway.*

While the vast majority of sites that feature teens are eighteen-plus legal, and in fact use women in their early twenties to act out 'cherry-popping' teens and schoolgirl fantasies, sometimes Marc had found that when he went 'site hopping' as he calls it (jumping from one pornography site to another via internal links), he had ended up viewing a site that made him feel uncomfortable – a site on which the girls had looked too young to him. Marc tries to rationalize this fact by telling himself that it is particularly difficult when viewing lots of Asian girls to tell their age. He tells himself that 'they' can often look quite young when they are well in to their twenties. You will hear about Marc's discomfort while viewing the Internet later, but right now he is using his own self-imposed rule.

Marc adds 'MILF' to the search bar.

Brunette in nylon pantyhose masturbates her **wet cunt**. He clicks the link like someone playing a fruit machine and – *This looks promising …*

The site fits his mood. Although he could easily masturbate again (and he would do so if he was at home), he rarely does that in his office. These days, it is unusual to find links that can still fire up what little sexual imagination and fantasy he has left – especially without 'hopping' to get there.

The screen is filled with thumbnail pictures of women holding their labia wide open while masturbating and fingering themselves, inserting dildos and other miscellaneous articles into their vaginas, plus a number where the picture shows a woman urinating. These are close-up, POV (point of view) shots, and he likes them.

10.46am It's almost time for the meeting now. *Just click through some of the links on the page.* New blogs – *Must take a quick look there.* Granny fucking … Nude grandmas … Sexy grannies … Granny fuck … Granny post – *MILF, not fucking GILF. If I had wanted GILF I'd have fucking put GILF in. I fucking hate the Internet.* Naked older women. (Clicks.) *Uhhhh! Puke; hope that keeps out of my dreams, nasty stuff wrinkles like that just there, uhhhh! What an old hag.* MILF porn … Busty MILF milk – *Bookmark that for later …* MILF nude – *B-I-N-G-O! Beautiful redhead! Oh yes, double vag.*

Marc uses the terms of the pornography industry like a professional. 'Double vag' is shorthand for 'double vaginal', an act in which two penises are simultaneously placed in one vagina. The image fills the screen. There are comments about the picture and links to other sites that Marc thinks look good. He's a little disappointed that the blogs are really just inter-page links rather than streaming video, but, like Busty MILF milk, Marc thinks they are worth bookmarking for later. It is 10.59am; he is late for his meeting.

●◄• •◄• •◄•

Marc has noticed that he is preoccupied with the Internet, sex and telephone chatlines. If he ever tries to cut down the time he spends on these activities he notices how moody, irritable and depressed he becomes. Louise and Marc discuss his excessive pornography usage. Mainly she has helped him to cut down his use of printed pornography. Louise has disliked printed pornography ever since she discovered her father using it in her sister's bedroom when she was six years old; she had never told anyone about what she had seen until she began to talk to Marc. There is much worse to come.

Between fucking, having sex and making love on the telephone and in the chatroom, Louise and Marc talk and connect deeply – although discussions about Marc's pornography difficulties often lead to rows, unhappiness and sulks from both parties. If Marc's wife Judy (JJ, as he calls her) challenges him about his collection of pornography or his demands in the bedroom, he becomes defensive – angry, even. He tells himself that pornography is just his hobby, that it is fun and that almost everyone uses pornography at some point these days. But inside he knows he is lying to himself. Inside he knows how ugly he feels and how unhappy and bored pornography makes him feel.

·◆· ·◆· ·◆·

So far, this has been a fairly typical morning for Marc in terms of his engagement with adult material. He woke up sexually aroused, like he has done almost every day for the last thirty-one years. Judy is frequently absent overnight because of work commitments, and on mornings when she is away Marc uses pornography before he gets out of bed. Since 2005 (when their home Internet connection became broadband and a router for wireless connection to his laptop was subsequently installed), if Judy is away, almost as soon as he is awake Marc tends to flick his computer open while still in bed and surf the net for porn. On other days, he sticks to older patterns of usage and takes a DVD from his pornography hoard (which, since 2003, has gradually replaced his VHS collection), and puts it in the player so he can watch men and women have sex on the large, now flatscreen, television in the bedroom. Masturbation has been part of Marc's morning ritual since before puberty. He can just remember when his orgasms had been strong, exciting, relaxing and quick. His orgasms used to be obtained by using still pictures in glossy thick-papered magazines. The pictures were of unselfconscious-looking women with pubic hair and natural breasts. Now, almost every time he masturbates it is a hardcore-pornography-driven marathon – an addiction, as *he* is starting to think of it. It is accompanied by a lack of meaning or fulfilment.

·•· ·•· ·•·

Marc's meeting will be a success today, despite his lateness. He will bask in this success for a short while before his mood falls, and as his mood flattens he will look at the Internet again. It will be 4.07pm when the pictures of the redhead 'receiving' double vaginal sex during his morning trawl of the World Wide Web will pass through his mind.

At 4.09pm Marc will set himself a task: *Starting from 'redhead', in how few moves can I get my search engine to deliver me some more double vag reds?* Marc will find it an easy task; once he adds 'babe' to the other search term his screen will be awash with sexual-ized redheads. He will find himself on RamRodBot.com at 4.12pm and a minute later he will be distracted by a fetish menu. He will click Watersports and he will remain at his desk for a further forty-five minutes looking at seemingly endless links and galleries and watch-ing one-minute clips of films where men and women urinate on each other and where European girls drink from Pyrex jugs full of their own urine.

At 5.15pm Marc will leave his office and drive home. At 6.15pm he will send Louise a text:

> **Loulou mwwwwwhhhhhh that's a big one**
> **from me. Cant speak tonight JJ home.**
> **Catch you early tomoz on the island**
> **mwwwhhh**

At 6.45pm Judy will return from a three-day European business trip. Marc and Judy will drink a little too much wine; they will fall asleep for a short while on the sofas facing each other in their living room; they will wake and think about having sex – 'welcome-home sex', like they used to have when they were in their twenties. But at 11.07pm they will simply ascend the staircase and fall into bed. At the end of the day, Marc will be glad not to have had to engage with Judy. He still loves his wife, but he does not feel like connecting with a real person right now. He will close his eyes for the last time today at 11.12pm and allow himself to float to his Island retreat with Louise: *Loulou, oh! Loulou.*

3 what men and women do

12 November 1976

Marc is sitting on the wooden steps that run out from the back of the fourth year juniors' classroom. It is a cold November day, but the sun is shining and Marc is busy pretending to smoke. He inhales on a white sweet cigarette stick tipped with a red-painted end to simulate the real, lighted thing. He exhales and enjoys the smoke-like effect his warm breath passing out from his lungs makes as it hits the cold surrounding air. He thinks he looks grown up – like his Uncle Aubert used to look. Aubert is currently reduced to life in a chair – emphysema restricting his lungs to the point of collapse.

Marc still knows little about the real world of adulthood. Cancer will stay in the shadows for another year, when it comes to life and takes Uncle Aubert. By then Marc will have learned much more about the grown-up world. Today will be an important day *en route*.

·•· ·•· ·•·

Marc shifts to the left of the classroom steps as Gareth, his best friend since nursery school, grins and swaggers towards him. Gareth is wearing a brand new green 'snorkel' parka. The amazing orange lining is peeping out as Gareth unzips his prized jacket and sits down beside him. Marc is quite jealous of Gareth's new 'snorkel'; it means he is now the only one of his and Gareth's friendship group without such a coat. He wants to punch Gareth for it. Marc hates feeling like an outsider.

'Where did you get that, Bushy?' Marc says.

'My brother got it for me; it's from his new job. He gave me some other stuff as well – you wanna see?'

'What's it going to cost?' replies Marc.

'It's really gross,' Gareth continues. 'Are you interested in seeing what men and women do when they are grown-ups?'

Although Marc is only ten years old, 'almost eleven', he would say he is quite ambivalent about sexual matters. In public he is cautious how other boys will view him over such things. He is acutely embarrassed by the nude artwork in the family home and he always slides the vase of flowers on the hallway side table to cover the naked breasts of the pictured woman before he opens the door to his friends. And yet, since he was five years old Marc has been experimenting with sex. Along with one of his sisters, Simone, who is two years older than him, Marc plays doctors and nurses games with their best out-of-school friends of the family – Ben and Adele. In their make-believe games Marc is the first to take off all his clothes and lie down on the 'examination table'. They take it in turns to examine each other. When Adele touches Marc's skin his penis begins to swell and he gets up from 'the operation' during the middle phase so as to strut around the room with his erection.

·•· ·•· ·•·

'You up for it, Frog?' asks Gareth for a second time? 'What men and women do when they are grown-ups?'

Marc nods and Gareth asks for his break-time Penguin biscuit in return for a rather tattered page, folded into quarters, which has been torn from a 'European magazine'. Marc walks across the playground to the boys' outside toilet block and locks himself in the cold sit-down cubicle. The toilet door does not reach to the floor or the ceiling so Marc is not guaranteed privacy in the space. He has to keep an ear out for others who will joyfully fling plastic bags full of water over the top to drench a stall's occupant.

Marc holds in his hand what feels like a passport to manhood. This is the typical rite of passage for boys of his generation. He unfolds the page that Gareth traded with him to reveal some black and white photographs in which a man and a woman who look like they have just left the pop group ABBA are having penetrative sex. Marc thinks the man's penis looks enormous; it is erect, he is very hairy and his penis is entering the shiny, wet and equally hairy vagina of the blonde woman. Marc feels a little scared that he will have to do this to a woman when he gets older. But he is glad for the confirmation that a penis does go in the front hole of a woman.

Until a moment ago he really had hoped that sex would be like the games he played in private. He wanted it to be about strutting around with his penis fully erect and engorged with blood, showing it off to the world and having girls stare at him; he wanted it to be about chasing girls around the room, like all those blondes and brunettes who ran around in *The Benny Hill Show*.

Marc looks at his own prepubescent penis. He wonders how it will ever get as big as the one in the picture. He becomes fascinated by how much hair will grow on and around it. He has adult thoughts but he is aware of how much of a child he is. He thinks of himself as James Bond, but he is a schoolboy with a bicycle rather than a secret agent with a prestigious car.

Marc is used to seeing his mother walk around naked in the mornings. She appears at ease moving between bedrooms and bathroom with nothing on. Marc is acutely awkward with her display. She enters his room clothes-free most mornings to pull back his curtains and wake him for school. Marc has seen both his older sisters naked. Simone is sprouting pubic hair and Veronique is already well developed. At almost sixteen years old, she is a woman. She has a mass of dark pubic hair and large breasts – bigger than their mother's. He sometimes pleads to use the toilet when Veronique is in the shower, then prankishly whips away the curtain to expose her. Until today he has not been certain why he does this.

The magazine pictures are the first time Marc has seen a mature male penis – and an erect one at that. His father is never glimpsed in a state other than fully clothed. On family holidays at the beach he remains in long trousers and a shirt, although he does roll up his sleeves. He seems uneasy with his body, with sex, with women. When he and Marc use the gents' urinals together, he always uses the cubical rather than standing next to his son, man alongside boy.

During the early to mid-1970s, there was no way that the testosterone-driven demands to worship Eros through accessing erotica, pornography and other sexual images could be achieved by a boy or young man on his own. However, older brothers, their friends and fathers who used pornography tended, at least in the cities, to be good suppliers. Bit by bit the masculine hormone-orientated mind of a boy reaching puberty could acquire access to a small portfolio of images worthy of masturbation, especially when it included a certain amount of liberation of young women in lingerie – courtesy of the underwear sections of pay-monthly catalogues such as Kays.

·•· ·•· ·•·

Marc folds the pornographic images back into his pocket and returns to the steps of the classroom. Gareth is waiting for him. Marc wants to take the pictures home with him, but to do so will almost certainly bring a ribbing from Gareth – and he does not know what trouble that could lead to.

While he sat in the stall and once he had got used to the pictures, he had felt a stirring in his guts and in his penis. It was not as strong as when Adele had touched his skin and certainly not as strong as when she had actually touched his penis the final time the quartet had met to play hospitals when Marc was seven years old. However, he knew he liked the feeling he had and he wanted to look at the pictures again.

'Gross, just like you said Bushy.'

'I knew you'd say that Frog, totally gross,' Gareth retorts.

Marc wishes as hard as he can for Gareth to say he can keep the pictures for the weekend. The bell-ringer stands in the playground and lunchtime is at an end. The pornographic images are in Marc's pocket and Mrs Freighter is already standing next to the boys on the classroom steps.

All the way through the next lesson Marc is imprinting in his mind the image of the penis entering the woman's vagina. His 'girlfriend', Sally, appears silly and young to him now. Yesterday, when he had held her hand by the monkey puzzle tree in the playground and when he had been dared to kiss her by Gareth, lips tightly closed, she had felt to him like Joanna Lumley as Purdy in *The New Avengers*.

In three days' time Sally and Marc will end their 'relationship'.

The rest of the afternoon is passing quickly, and at final play of the day Gareth asks Marc to hand back the page full of pictures. Given there is no real opportunity for Gareth to embarrass Marc this late in the day, Marc asks to keep hold of them: 'I'm going to Ben's tomorrow, and he might cough up 10 pence to look at that gross stuff. I'll split the cash with you 50:50 if he does.'

'How will I know if he does or not? You could rip me off.'

'You dill; I'm not goin' to rip my friend off am I – partners; yeah partners in crime!'

Gareth whistles the theme tune to *The Sweeney*.

Marc's heart is beating really fast. It's true that he might make a few pence selling Ben a look at the pictures tomorrow, but there is no way anyone other than him will be having the pictures tonight.

'Packing up now, class,' says Mrs Freighter, 'Girls, chairs on tables please. Now boys.'

The class stands silently waiting for the day's prefect to ring the bell. A door opens into the main hall that all the classrooms surround. The clapper of the bell makes a muffled sound as the prefect's hand wraps around it. Like Pavlov's dogs, 4F are attuned to this noise. Three or four steps on the highly polished parquet floor will echo in the Victorian hall before the prefect does her work and rings out the sweet sound of going home.

Marc is released. He raises a hand to Gareth: 'See you Sunday Bushy.'

'Bring the cash, Frogger.'

Marc loves Fridays. Friday night is Cubs, a different group of boys, the lovely Akela who has a big bust, really blonde hair and smells of a wonderful mix of Peter Stuyvesant cigarettes and the perfume counter of a department store. Marc will spend the first few pence of his pocket money on the way home from the Cub meeting; greasy batter scraps from the chip shop will fill his 'hollow legs', followed by fruit

Polos that he will purchase from the off licence at the top of the hill. He will check in the phone box on the corner by the school for any change that has been forgotten, and Veronique will let him in at home when he arrives – hot, tired and happy. Veronique and Simone will try to boss him about as he uses the sofa as a trampoline while watching the television. But tonight they will fail to have any power over him. He has seen that women are the ones who are penetrated. He has seen that men are dominant. Despite the fact it is his mother who bullies and hits him, and despite the bra-burning he has heard of in the news, he has seen that women lie down and let men penetrate their vaginas – and there is nothing they can do about it. It is the way of the world.

The house is quiet as Marc climbs into bed that night. His mother and father are still out and Veronique is in charge. He has gone to bed without a fuss. Quietly, he looks at the borrowed porn. He normally masturbates when he wakes up in the morning but today his sexual charge is greater. He turns himself around on the bed, hangs his head over the end and begins to rubs himself against the sheets. He keeps his gaze away from as much of the penis and testicles of the male porn model as he can. He focuses his attention on the vagina and the breasts of the bubbly looking blonde. A few seconds of rubbing and he orgasms a huge pulsing wave of sexual excitement. He folds the magazine page and slides it between the cover and the dust jacket of a hardback book on his shelf. He closes his eyes. Sleep approaches quickly; he has just enough time to think back to when Adele stroked his penis.

Tomorrow Marc will arrive at Ben's house at 9.30am. Adele will open the door to him. She is almost fourteen years old now and her strawberry blonde hair will shine in the morning light. Marc will see how much of a woman she is becoming. Her cheesecloth top and her jeans. He will feel like a little boy, but his mind will think sexual thoughts about her – what she might look like now without her clothes on, her breasts and her pubic hair. Her frame is willowy and mysterious. As he considers these things, he will carry on talking to Ben.

Adele is still not like the sisters of Marc's other friends. She is nice to him. She mothers him slightly. She finds him cute. In the summer holiday of her first year at university, she will have sex with him. She will be the one who takes his virginity away from him on a joint family camping holiday in Cornwall.

Ben will not be interested in the pictures Marc is 'pimping'. He will think there are much better things to do than look at grown-up women. He'd rather listen to Status Quo than examine pictures of people who look like ABBA having sex.

Later in the evening, when the rest of his family are watching television, Marc will go to his bedroom and trace the different images of the couple having sex as best as he can. For the next few weeks this will be his masturbation fodder.

On Sunday morning at church, Marc will think it is better to lie to Gareth about Ben. He will tell him how Ben thought the same of the pictures as they did: 'Gross.' He will pay him 5 pence from his own pocket money, pretending it is a 50:50 deal and, very quietly when no one is looking, he will hand the pictures back.

4 regressed

29 March 2007

Three months from today, Marc will enter therapy. In his secret online conversations with Louise he feels anxious. The anxiety drives him to evermore frequent masturbation both on his own and while having cybersex with Louise. He does not know where to turn, so he talks to her.

There is much in the strange and unfolding relationship between Marc and Louise that in the psychotherapy profession is referred to as a *parallel process*. Marc finds in her personal social history the very same anxiety he feels from his own. They manifest this anxiety differently, but they both unconsciously recognize themselves in the other – the you in me.

Marc experiences Louise as a very kind person. What he does not see is that she is also a deeply damaged human being who is unable to live out a sexual or romantic life in the real world. What Marc does not see is that *he* is a deeply damaged human being, and one in whom the damage is unable to be repaired all the time he is living his life in such a desensitized manner. Marc will discover more of his parallel process with Louise when he enters therapy.

.•. .•. .•.

Louise was eighteen when she married her first husband, Mick. He was a handsome man, an alcoholic and a bully. Louise tried hard to support Mick, but nine months after her wedding she was being beaten to the floor for the fourth time in their marriage by the man who said he loved her and would never do this to her again. Her injuries included a broken arm and internal bleeding. She spent three days in hospital.

.•. .•. .•.

Marc is deeply confused by his feelings towards Louise. She enjoys the level of dependency he has on her. She enjoys the power. Nothing makes any sense.

7.05pm Marc goes to his wardrobe drawer and fully pulls it out of its housing. He fishes to the left-hand side, catches the carpet with his finger and thumb, and peels it off the floorboards. He is able to flick up one floorboard, then put his hand into the crevice below. He can feel two A4 envelopes with his fingertips; this is his secret stash of pornography.

Almost prone on the floor, he wonders why he still does this. He has pornographic magazines in his bedside drawer and Judy knows about them – although Marc does not know that Judy regularly checks to see which ones he is buying. From time to time she will use some of the lesbian images when she masturbates on her own. But Marc no longer buys the sorts of magazines she really used to enjoy.

During the 1990s *Fiesta*, *Escort* and *Mayfair* were his regular purchases, and Marc and Judy looked at them together before they had sex or masturbated each other. During a period of frenetic buying after the UK censorship laws were relaxed in July 2000, Marc became much more secretive about his pornography. He and Judy stopped reading it together. Judy noticed the way these magazines began to show mainly hardcore penetrative sex. She finds this boring. They lack the ability to stimulate her imagination, but sometimes Marc buys US titles like *40MILF+* and *Naughty Slut* and Judy can again enjoy the stories and letters like before, only now she takes herself to the bathroom, since through pornography she has learned enough about female ejaculation that she is now able to let herself gush into the toilet bowl.

The envelopes Marc has just retrieved from under the floorboards are full of the images he would not want Judy to know he looked at; he is uncertain about many of them himself. *Perhaps*, he thinks as he undresses and lies down on the bed, *I don't need these any more.*

For a moment Marc feels guilty about the way he is betraying Judy with Louise. For a moment he feels guilty about the fact that although he has severely cut down his use of printed pornography, he has not given it up, which is what he has told Louise he has done. *Loulou who found her father masturbating in her older sister's bedroom, sniffing* … He pushes the thought from his mind, and turns over, face down looking towards the floor, head hanging off the end of the bed. As he hardens he remembers that this is how he learned to masturbate as a child, rubbing his penis on the sheets until he orgasmed. For the moment he has forgotten that the first time he did this was when he borrowed his very first pornographic images from his friend Gareth. He does remember how he used to masturbate like this thinking about Miss Pringle, one of his primary school teachers, spanking his bare buttocks with a wooden ruler. It is when he reached puberty and started to ejaculate at orgasm that he finally learned how to masturbate like the other boys did, with his hand wrapped around the shaft of his penis.

Right now, Marc is regressed. He is trying to recreate something of the excitement of his early experience with pornography. He is trying to be a teenager, younger even. He thinks of the simplicity of Miss Pringle's mini-skirt revealing her strong thighs. He wants her attention. He wants her to call him to the corner and stand with his back to the class. He wants to be humiliated.

The envelopes Marc has just retrieved are full of pictures torn from magazines, just like when he had first seen pornographic images. This is his R-18 portfolio, gleaned from various sources just like it was in the 1970s.

Marc begins with the softer images – the ones with pretence that the models are real girls next door.

Lilly, Belfast, 22 years old, shopworker, 8 stone 5 pounds, 32B cup, 5 ft 6 ins

Lilly thinks her toys are an addiction now …

When I began, I slipped into a sex shop and bought this vibe for my little clitty. Then I got a much bigger one for my pussy. After I first used it inside my bottom I got another one specifically for anal workouts. Now I like a fist …

Lilly your hair is so beautiful. God, I wish I could get my tongue to your big lips … Why are you putting your hand down your panties, you naughty girl? Finger in your arsehole already … the way your mouth is open … those two vibes in your holes …

Nadine, Sydney, Australia, 21 years old, student, 9 stone 8 pounds, 34C cup, 5 ft 4 ins

So why did she pose?

For the money, of course. I want to get my own car and my shitty job pays peanuts …

You hot chubby bitch … nice round arse. Walk towards me. Let me see that gorgeous round tummy of yours … Those lips just need to be pulled a little wider, ummmh; your puckered hole is opening as well. I bet you've just been letting your boyfriend fuck you in that hole …

Patti …

Two guys, one bitch

Not today … not today Patti. You know I had you last time. If you ask me I'll have to tie you down to the bench again, bind your wrists and then beat your arse like he is doing to you now. Yes you bitch, I'll whip you again; I'll whip you and then use that cane in the corner on your bare, stretched-out arse. I'll gag you with your used panties, whip you, beat you, cane you until you squirt, 'til you plead and cry and the tears run down your cheeks … whip you until the welts rise and you bruise.

Unconsciously, Marc is remembering from his childhood parts of an attack on him – one of the many beatings he took and the humiliations he withstood.

Justine, hometown, Philadelphia, age 26

Cum in my face. Piss all over my big tits. Spit in my pussy. I can take it. I love the feeling of all the hot fluid washing over …

Those panties being pulled out of your hole … stretching your cheeks … wish I was that bar of soap …

I can feel all that warm piss cascading over my tits, almost at the point of no control …

I can feel all that warm piss, that warm piss …

Marc turns over the page to an image of a man in leather trousers lying underneath a woman's legs. She is urinating into his open mouth.

… that warm piss, I can feel all that warm piss … piss … piss …

Marc ejaculates onto the piece of cloth he has laid over the sheets that he's been rubbing himself against. He imagines Miss Pringle urinating on him, humiliating him and herself in front of an audience. He imagines Louise tied to a chair as he sits on the floor in front of her pushing on her lower abdomen until an arc of urine is forced out of her and into his open mouth. He feels physically hot but these are not the 'good old times' he has tried to recreate. He has not ejaculated quickly. It has not had that hard urgency he craves. He simply oozes a faint dribble of sperm by comparison to his youth. And there is this empty, even guilty, feeling.

Arranging the magazine pages back into a pile Marc wipes his penis, abdomen and the piece of cloth dry of his sperm. He slides the pages back into the envelope and returns them once more to the secret hiding place. Marc goes to the bathroom to clean himself up.

Judy is working away again. Tonight she will be sleeping in a hotel in Barcelona. Marc thinks of her. He picks up the phone and dials. 'Hello sexy, mwhhh. Have you had a good day?' he asks.

'Oh Marc, I'm right in the middle of something. Can I phone you back in about an hour?' It is 8.26pm.

'I was just going to take a shower and then probably head off to bed. I've got a really early start tomorrow. I'm meeting Nick in Manchester at 11am.'

'You'll be up bloody early then,' Judy says.

'I'll be leaving the house about 5.30 otherwise the next train cuts it way too fine for me to get to the meeting. When are you back?' asks Marc.

'Tuesday sweet; I'll see you then. Mwh.'

Marc feels empty again.

'Okay, see you on Tuesday. I'll phone you tomorrow.'

'Okay, love, but don't phone 'til late. I'm with a client in the evening,' Judy replies.

'Night …' says Marc, '… sweet dreams, don't let the bed bugs bite.'

Judy laughs. 'Don't let the bed bugs bite, mwh, later.' She hangs up.

Marc continues to feel empty. He switches the SIM card in his mobile and dials another number. 'Hello sexy, mwhhh. Have you had a good day?'

'Oh baby, oh! mwh – hang on a minute, there's a call coming through.' Louise puts her phone on the secrecy function for a moment. She does not like Marc to hear her working. She hates that he might think he is still a punter, that she is turning him a trick. It has felt like this from the very first call they had on the 09 premium rate number.

Marc's mobile vibrates alerting him to a new text message:

> **Soz darlin mad er 2nite, hang up mob.**
> **dont wste moni. Go 2 the island – writ a**
> **poem 4u. Talk there.**

Marc still feels empty. He hangs up. An outsider again, abandoned, he is motionless for a few moments. His mind is totally silent. He is taken over by an image: he sees himself standing in the middle of a frozen lake; it is snowing and he is naked, standing in bare feet. It's a total white-out. His eyes are crying but he can't feel anything. His heart is empty. Marc wants to reach out and touch someone. He wants Louise; he wants Judy; he wants Alison, Emma, Carolyn, Jayne, Rebecca, Adele … He picks up his mobile phone again and dials a number he has memorized.

'I have to tell you that FYS Ltd provides this service and all calls are recorded for your protection and to comply with ICSTIS regulations … calls cost 35 pence per min …'

Marc presses 3: 'Please enter the PIN of the girl of your choice.'

Marc taps in 37672.

'I'm sorry, the girl you have chosen is currently on a call. Please enter the PIN of the girl of your choice.'

Again Marc taps 37672 and again the reply: 'I'm sorry the girl you have chosen is currently on a call.'

Fuck you Loulou, fuck you bitch.

Tears continue to roll down Marc's face, but he feels nothing.

It is 9.01pm and Marc picks up the phone once more. He can hardly see the numbers on the pad. He dials 08457 909090. The phone rings three times before it is picked up. A softly spoken man answers: 'Samaritans. Can I help?' Marc is silent; he is still lost in his internal white space. He does not know how long he is silent, but the man speaks to him again: 'I'm here.' He is silent again and then: 'How are you doing? I'm still here.'

Seconds later, Marc puts down the phone.

5 aural sex

Marc looks at his watch: 7.03pm. He is about to have aural sex with a woman he has never spoken to. Unlike the hundreds of women he has had telephone sex with in the past, Marc will make a deep connection with the operator who picks up the phone to him this evening.

The company Marc currently uses to make his phone sex calls has four main shifts per day, each of them lasting six hours. The shifts change at 7am, 1pm, 7pm and 1am. The company sometimes allows its female operators to log in and out for shorter shifts during busy periods, particularly around the 7pm changeover time.

He lifts the receiver.

This is like deciding to go out for a pleasure drive in the middle of the rush hour.

Although it is counter-intuitive to make a call at the busiest point in the day, he also knows the advantages. The women are normally at their most positive and receptive at the start of the shift; there is also the maximum number of operators on line to choose from. When Marc phones during the day's quiet points most of the women's voices are familiar ones, and this normally takes away from a call the edge and excitement.

⋯ ⋯ ⋯

'I have to tell you that FYS Ltd provides this service and all calls are recorded to comply with ICSTIS phone regulations and for your protection. Calls cost 65 pence per minute and will appear on your bill. You must be the bill payer or have the bill payer's permission and be eighteen or over to use this service. We may send you promotional messages in response to this call.'

The rather austere female voiceover changes to a more excited 'tarty' vocal.

'This is the shortest intro on any UK sex line, so let's get straight down to the hot and horny, live, one-to-one sex. You are about to be connected to the girl of your dreams, so don't hang up; unzip your trousers and get your cock in your hand for the phone fuck of a lifetime.'

A third recorded voice speaks to Marc.

'Press 1 for the first available hottie; press 2 to hear the girls introduce themselves; or press 3 if you already know the PIN number of the babe you'd like to speak to.'

Marc presses 2. The woman's voice continues …

'In a moment you will hear a list of the beautiful girls waiting to talk to you on line right now. When you hear a girl's introduction that you like, press any key while she is speaking and you'll be put right through to her. If you miss the lovely lady then don't worry as the list will play again, or press the star key to return to the main menu.'

A sexy West Country voice speaks.

'Hi guys, my name's Lucy and I'm, well, rather juicy,' she giggles in a fake teenage sort of manner. 'I'm only five foot one and I'm very attractive with my deep brown eyes and curly brunette hair. I have a gorgeous sexy figure with curves in all the right places. I'm a warm, chatty, mature lady and very broad minded – so, if you'd like a nice friendly chat or some fun between my thirty-six double Ds' – she giggles once more – 'then please feel free to call me.'

The next woman in the list speaks.

'Hi, I'm Kiki and I have really long blonde hair and twinkling green eyes with a lovely fresh complexion. I've just got out of the shower and now I'm feeling really hot and horny. So guys, come on over because we can have lots of fun together – right now.'

⋅◆⋅ ⋅◆⋅ ⋅◆⋅

When it's busy on the chatline, Marc knows it's pointless trying to get connected to one of the women played early in the recorded list of available operators. They will already have been connected either to someone who knows their PIN and has been waiting for them to come on shift or to someone who presses 1 for the first available girl while Marc is still listening to the woman's introduction.

Marc uses the telephone line often enough to know all the regular women by their introductions. Having used this particular line (in its various incarnations) for years he has either already spoken to most of the women or not fancied making contact with the others. Therefore, although it is expensive to listen all the way through the complete list of available operators, by doing so he is aware when new women join the company. If there are no new operators, he can then make a selection, via a PIN, of the woman he wants to speak with during that call.

⊶⋅ ⊶⋅ ⊶⋅

'Hi, my name's Loulou,' says a bubbly London voice. 'If you love watersports and want to talk to a more mature lady …' The phone rings twice before Louise picks the receiver up.

⊶⋅ ⊶⋅ ⊶⋅

Louise is a forty year-old single mother with two children: Amy has just had her sixteenth birthday and lives at home with Louise; David, nineteen, has recently left home to live with his African-Caribbean boyfriend.

Life is a financial roller-coaster for Louise. She has two failed and abusive marriages behind her. As a child she used to go to Sunday school; she used to be a Christian but God let her down. He gave her a pervert for a father and a depressed, abusive mad woman for a mother. In her life she has been beaten up, psychologically abused and raped numerous times. She does not like men very much. Mainly they revolt her. Working on a telephone sex chatline does little if anything to improve her opinion. When she lies in the bath trying to feel warm and clean, she still thinks there must be some kind men in the world and she dreams of meeting one.

Louise will tell Marc that when she last had some therapy her therapist tried to put her in a box. She wanted to tell the therapist to 'fuck off' nearly every session; she wanted to tell him she was a human being, not a set of symptoms. She was angry with him because he took her extremely hard-earned money and he wouldn't give her what she wanted – she wanted him to hug her, not analyse her. When she tried to tell him that she loved him, he just mentioned more labels; he thought she might be displaying a number of features of a 'borderline personality disorder'. As she got closer to him, trusted him, he did what every man has done to her: he rejected her. Her therapist suggested a referral to another psychotherapist who had more experience with borderline patients as well as the difficulties she was talking about with regard to her traumatic sexual past.

Louise stopped taking the drugs her GP had prescribed. She arranged a holiday for her children with their uncle and she drove to Beachy Head where she intended to jump. She will tell Marc about the details of that late-summer evening – how very easy it would have been for her to end it all, save for a woman who witnessed her distressed state and who calmly approached and spoke to her. Louise didn't jump. She heard the woman's words, and she didn't jump.

Right now in life, Louise enjoys the power she thinks she has over men. In her work time she has the power to make them orgasm or to frustrate them. Most importantly no man on the telephone line can ever invade her personal space.

⁘⁘ ⁘⁘ ⁘⁘

'Hello,' says the warm and friendly voice at the end of the phone.

'Hi,' Marc replies.

'How you doing there? You alright?' Louise says.

'I'm not too bad,' replies Marc.

Marc's opening dialogues are always like this. He wants to see if the woman will take the lead or whether she wants him to do the work. He hates women who simply follow a script from the start or who watch television at the same time as they are working. He knows there are reasons why they do this. He also knows it's nothing personal. He knows these things because he likes to carry on talking after he has orgasmed. In the post-masturbatory space, the women are aware he is really communicating with them. They understand it's genuine rather than as a result of him being turned on. This makes the operators remarkably honest and open.

'My name's Matt,' he says.

'Have we spoken before, Matt? I'm sure I recognize your voice.'

Marc laughs. 'I've just got one of those voices.'

Louise giggles back. 'You sound absolutely lovely, Matt – who I have never spoken to before!' She giggles again.

There is a strong charge instantly for Marc in this conversation.

'And what's your name?'

'Loulou,' she says. 'Okay Matt, tell me a little about you then.'

Marc has a description he always uses when he is on line. He does not know why he does not describe himself as he is, but he does not.

'I've got short blonde hair, blue eyes, I'm about six foot two inches, fifteen and a half stone and a good hard six inches.'

'Ohh! Very nice,' Louise coos back.

'And how about Loulou?' Marc asks.

'Well, I guess you'd call me petite, but with the right curves. I'm only a little 'un, about five foot two,' she says, 'but you can always stick a pair of high heels on me if you don't want to bend down to catch my beautiful red lips.' They both laugh out loud together. As Louise draws in her breath she continues. 'I'm brunette, I've got big green eyes and I'm 32C, 28, 36 – so petite but with real woman's hips,' she says, impersonating Mae West.

'Ooh, a nice round bottom,' Marc says, 'just how a lady's bottom should be.'

'It's a nice spankable round bottom, too,' Louise continues. 'I do like a nice bit of spanking, I must admit …' (she pauses while Marc fills the gap with an appreciative rumble) '… but we could think of something else – if sir likes?'

God, you know full well where I want to go already don't you Loulou?

Marc begins his descent into his erotic space. He is thinking of the reference to watersports he heard in the short snippet of Louise's introduction before he pressed a number on his keypad to connect to her.

Let's not go too fast right now. Let's not spoil the journey Loulou can serve up.

'Ooh, what other things do you like to do you naughty girl?' Marc asks.

An instant reply fires back: 'Everything.'

Louise is surprised by her own feelings during this call. It is rare for her to feel turned on in a conversation, and if she ever does it is usually something that takes a long time.

'That's a dangerous thing to say to me,' Marc parries.

'Everything,' she repeats. 'I'm an open-minded sort of girl and I think you can hear I'm not a teenager, so I've had chance to get up to an awful lot of different things in the bedroom.'

'So how old are you, darling?' Marc asks.

'Life begins at …' she says.

And Marc replies, '… forty. Snap!'

'I hope you are young at heart Matt, like me. I can tell you're a sexy beast – I'm hoping you are anyway. Tell me, what are you into? I bet you've tried a few things.'

Marc is in his element; he feels lightheaded, intoxicated. He has a huge amount of credit on his mobile phone, he has a very engaging and willing woman to talk to, and she is leading him on to talk about what *he* wants rather than switching off or holding him back. His penis is rigid as he strokes it with the fingers of his right hand.

'When you get to our age you have tried many things,' he replies. He is teasing *her*, putting the ball back in her court.

'I've experimented with most things, you know,' Louise says.

'Like?' Marc asks.

Although Louise is very good at this game, she feels less in control than normal and she is feeling more than a little erotic charge in herself.

'I'll give you a few guesses,' she bats back.

⋅◆⋅ ⋅◆⋅ ⋅◆⋅

The average phone sex session lasts twenty minutes for Marc. He is just four minutes two seconds into this one and already he can feel the first stirring of his orgasm. Marc finds it difficult to masturbate and talk, so in order to dampen his ardour he gives in to Louise's game.

'Come on Matt, what things have you tried, tested and enjoyed in the bedroom – or anywhere else?' She giggles again.

'I particularly like anal,' Marc volunteers.

'Doooo you?' Louise elongates the words in order to convey her interest and growing excitement. 'Giving, receiving or both?' she continues.

'I've done both,' Marc replies 'but I must say I like to give it the most. I also like watersports but I like receiving that, not giving it.'

As Marc speaks, Louise takes shorthand notes on a new page of a notebook. She has written today's date, her caller's name and the time of the call. As always, Louise is executing her job in a highly professional manner, but her mind is racing. Her sexual feelings are complex and despite the fact she works in the sex industry, personally she feels quite a lot of shame where her own sexual fantasies are concerned. Marc is already beginning to plug in to some of her own desires, and urinating on a man, degrading him, is a prime masturbation fantasy for her. But she can only get pleasure from such fantasies when she also imagines that she herself has just been violated or humiliated.

'So,' Louise asks, 'out of the two' (this question is just for her own pleasure) 'would you say you were submissive rather than dominant?'

'No,' Marc replies. 'I'm probably quite dominant but with watersports it's the other way around.'

The sexual pressure Marc is feeling is enormous. A buzzing sensation takes over his whole body.

This is like fucking myself; there must be a direct link between my brain and Loulou's.

And yet very little has really been said. What Marc is aware of is that a script is being written for him as he talks. Louise is busy constructing him a play, and he is about to become one of two main characters in it. He will be playing himself; the only disguise he will have is that of the description he gave Louise at the beginning of the phone conversation. In all other ways he will be naked.

'Well this is getting interesting,' Louise says. 'Most of the people I speak to enjoy being dominated but I'm just like you: I switch; I enjoy both. So this should be fun for you and fun for me.'

Louise is aware that she has now become very aroused. She is rubbing her clitoris through her underwear. She does not like to touch her bare genitals unless she has to – although she finds it much easier to touch herself when 'performing' for a sexual partner.

·•· ·•· ·•·

When Louise was a child, her mother, who meted out severe punishments, made it very clear that a girl should never touch her own genitals. One night, when she was caught with her hands below the bed sheets, her mother pulled her out of the bed, stripped her of all her clothing and made her stand on the freezing landing of their family home for an hour – hands tight to her outer thighs, not moving. Even when that ordeal was over, her mother made her sleep on top of the bed sheets (with her nightclothes on) for the rest of the week.

There are other reasons too. Abuse has led Louise to a number of rituals, including particular ones that concern her underwear.

·•· ·•· ·•·

'I do like it when a man knows how to dominate me correctly.'

'Well, let's begin with me being your master for a bit, then.'

'Oh master, I'm getting more excited as every second passes.'

'It might be a real mix,' Marc says, not quite knowing how the mood will take him. 'Let's just start with you kneeling down in front of me.'

'Okay.'

'I'm pulling your hair out of its knot and letting it fall around your shoulders …'

'A-ha.'

'… while I unzip my fly and pull out my cock.'

'A-ha.'

'I make you put your hands behind your back and then I fasten them with Velcro straps.'

'A-ha.'

Louise continues to masturbate herself. There is something about Marc's manner that makes her want to surrender to him. His voice is soft, sexy, well educated.

'I'm feeding my cock into your mouth. You have to hold your mouth wide open and in a perfect "O" shape.'

Louise coughs and splutters like a porn star receiving a deep throat penetration.

'And now I'm feeding it deep into the back of your throat.'

Louise coughs more and breathes heavily, making choking sounds.

We've only just begun; I'm not some premature ejaculator about to spurt out on you. You are in for a ride, bitch!

'And then I pull it out of your mouth and look at your face in front of me and I pull you up from your knees and I push you over the end of the bed. I unzip your skirt and I pull it down and then I roughly pull your panties down, un-Velcro your wrists and instruct you to take your hands behind you …'

The noises Louise makes are almost scaring her. She feels like she is with Marc in her own bedroom. She desperately wants him to get this right for *her*. She wants him to use her so that she can humiliate him.

'… and spread your cheeks open as wide as you can for me.'

'Oh, God, oh, no,' Louise moans out.

'What are you complaining at, whore?' Marc snaps. 'Have I given you permission to speak?'

'No master … oh, sorry master … but oh … oh … God, I've never done it like this before; please don't do this to me, not like this.'

Louise is leading Marc not just through his own script towards anal sex but towards her own desire to be raped (anally on this occasion) and then to recover from this torment through humiliating her rapist later by urinating on him.

'What is wrong with you bitch, if you don't know what I'm going to do to you?'

'It's just that you are asking me pull my cheeks open.'

'Yes!' Marc snaps at Louise.

'What are you going to do?' she asks.

Marc has in mind his role of master and is ready to play it. However, Louise is inviting him somewhere he is not sure he has been before. He is prepared to go with the flow. *I should tell her not to answer her master back. I should take a cane and beat her for her insubordination.*

'I want you to tell me what you *think* I'm going to do,' Marc snaps back at Louise.

Louise could get in trouble with her company if she goes too far towards her own fantasy of rape and degradation – how she would really want it done to her. She opts to revert to the script she had planned for Marc.

'You're not going to slide that massive cock up my tiny tight little arse are you?' she says.

'Of course I'm going to. I'm going to bugger you, you stupid little tart.'

'Oh! Please, I've never been buggered before sir.'

'Well you are about to get buggered now.'

'Oh please, master have mercy, oh please, I'm scared,' Louise continues.

The next five minutes are filled with Marc and Louise playing out their own fantasies within each other's fantasy. As if creating their own passage drawn from Pauline Réage's classic 1950s sado-masochistic novel *The Story of O*, Marc has made Louise plead not to be buggered, has made her cry from the spanking and the whipping he has meted out, and when she has opened up her anus with a butt plug and he has proved to her that his 'massive cock *will* fit into her tiny tight little arse', they switch roles.

Marc signals the change, 'Now what can I do to make that gaping arsehole feel better?'

Louise has been hoping for, awaiting the switch. 'Lick it!' she says in a stern voice.

Marc has not quite given up the dominant role, 'Lick what?'

'My arsehole, you piece of shit.'

Marc taunts Louise, 'Oooh! Piece of shit am I? That's original.'

'A piece of shit to lick my shit-hole. Now shut the fuck up, you impotent cocksucker, and lay back down on the bed …'

Louise is grabbing the power well and at the same time Marc is reaching his climax.

'I'm going to pee on you now. You are going to lie still while I go to the toilet on you, piss all over you. I'm going to soak you in my golden shower and you are going to have to drink me down.'

There is an orgasmic grunt from Marc as he ejaculates.

Louise does not stop talking; she is interested in the final moments of what she can have for herself. The sound of Marc's climax signals to her that he may well be about to put the phone down. Once satisfied, men mostly hang up within moments of orgasm, not even polite enough to thank the woman who has just done the aural pleasuring.

'My piss is washing over your chest; I'm arcing my love nectar at your balls and then washing it up your body and over your face. I slap an expanding ring in your mouth and it holds your lips open. I aim my piss into your mouth and gravity makes you swallow my burning hot fluid. I'm standing on the bed, pissing over you; you'll spend all night chained to the wet bed, smelling my liquid, the liquid that burns your skin and makes you sore while you try and think about something other than your mistress. Now, what about this butt plug? I think we'll have it up *your* arse,' Louise says, bringing herself back from the brink of orgasm – remembering that she is being paid to look after her client.

Marc laughs out loud. 'No! Not now, I've come!' Louise joins in – a sexy, chesty laugh.

'There we go,' Marc says.

'Fuck, you're lovely …' Louise replies. 'Can I give you my PIN number?' she almost babbles, expecting Marc to hang up any second.

'You bloody well can!' he says. 'I was worried you might not want to.'

'Oooh goodie, 37672. I've got to say, you have been the best call of the day and I have had loads.'

Marc laughs out loud again. He has heard this before from the women he talks to.

'No seriously, in fact you are the best caller I've had since I moved to this line.'

'You flatter me madam. Fuck, you are one of the best yourself. No, you are *the* best – and believe me I have made thousands of calls over the years.'

Louise feels warm inside, orgasmic without having climaxed, but she is also uncomfortable that this stranger could make her feel quite this way.

Marc leans over to his iPod resting in its speaker system and flicks it on. Louise is surprised he's still on the line. *Why hasn't he gone?* She can't hear the track very well – but she can distinguish a female artist singing something quite nice.

'You playing our song?' she giggles.

'If I was with you there right now, I'd pull you close to me, spoon you, kiss you on the back of the neck, slowly, very slowly working my way down your body, making your spine tingle as I move lower towards your cheeks …'

Marc can hear Louise's breathing deepen and become more intense.

'Loulou, your skin is so soft, you smell sweet, let me taste your pussy, let me lick you from your clit to your arse, let me taste your sweet juice …'

Marc is now making love to Louise; he is considerate, sensual, erotic, pulling her this way, letting her down only to build again. In the next ten minutes Louise hardly utters a word; she strokes herself, gently at first but Marc's low comforting voice helps her to build momentum. Just as she is about to erupt in orgasm she fears Marc will cut the call. She almost hopes he will leave her in that moment of ecstasy, abandon her so she can hate him, hate him for what he is doing to her. But he does not. Marc's goal is to make this professional sexline worker really connect with him, like she has made him connect with her. By the time Louise finally has her orgasm, Marc is hard again himself.

'I feel like I've been electrocuted,' Louise pants as she begins to be able to talk again.

'I'm glad; you did say I was the best call you've had on this line.'

'You arrogant shit!' she pants at him.

'And your point is …?'

'You were fucking amazing … tell me what you look like again … oh no, you'll just spoil it … if you can do this for me as a woman … I know you are going to be five foot one, fifteen stone and bald and have spots – whatever you say.'

'Ah! My secret is out – Adieu, sweet Amaryllis, adieu.'

'What the fuck does that mean?' asks Louise.

'Goodbye my flower – if you like, you will discover more from me another day, mwwhhh,' Marc kisses the phone.

'Oh! Goodnight sir, I send you a fond farewell then.' She giggles once more. 'Do you think we could do it in an Elizabethan four-poster bed next time?'

'You will have to wait and see,' Marc says. 'Goodnight, mwwhhh.'

'Goodnight, you *will* phone again?' Louise hates herself for that last comment; *pathetic* she thinks. 'Mwwhh.'

Marc presses the end-of-call key. He smiles and enjoys the strange warm feeling he has received from Louise. He is ready to masturbate once more.

6 welcome to our island

13 December 2006

Marc reaches over to the shelf above his desk in his study and draws down a hardback book. Unpeeling the dust jacket, he detaches a SIM card that is stuck to the surface of the book cover with some black vinyl tape. He flips the back off his mobile and exchanges the SIM card in the phone. He punches in a telephone number. The number rings …

'I have to tell you that FYS Ltd provides this service and all calls are recorded for your protection …'

·•· ·•· ·•·

Marc has always been very careful not to be discovered using tele-phone sexlines. One of his fears is that Judy will check the memory of his mobile phone if she becomes suspicious of him for any reason – it's what he might do to her. Therefore, Marc uses a separate SIM card when he makes sex calls and his ritual at the end of a conversation is to clear the entire memory of the phone so that there is no record of whom he has rung – it is an unregistered, pay-as-you-go card with nothing stored on it.

When Marc began to use 0898 telephone numbers for sexual pleas-ure they were what he now thinks of as 'rip-off' recorded messages that promised 'dirty sex' but were in fact still very much the product of the naughty seaside postcard, slap-and-tickle titillation tradition of British erotic history. In May 1989 all this changed when he used his first live sex chatline.

Marc has long forgotten the peripheral detail about sexline call charges and that they were once metered as peak or off-peak tariffs. He has now forgotten what year 0898 numbers changed to 09 prefix lines, and he can't even remember when he stopped using telephone boxes and began to use a mobile phone instead.

Marc's conversations with Louise have been going on for eleven months. As he lies in bed this morning fantasizing about his next conversation with her, it raised an echo of the excitement calls used to have in the pre-digital telephone era when he would actually have to speak to an operator who 'cleared' him through to a girl – like a prostitute's 'maid'. Speaking to the maid had an erotic taboo of its own for him. The maid knew that he was sexually excited making the call but there was a beautifully British politeness and formality to the clearing process. Marc would often ask the maid if he could talk to *her* rather than one of the girls since, 'you sound so sweet and gentle and I bet you're very attractive yourself'. Marc enjoyed breaking the 'rules'; his attempts at subverting the process made him more intensely aroused. He was making something formal 'dirty'. With good manners the women always refused him, but occasionally he managed to raise a laugh from one of the maids, and this he liked. It had made the process be between two real people. These times are almost two decades ago now, a distant part of Marc's pornized life.

··· ··· ···

'Press 1 for the first available operator; press 2 to hear the girls introduce themselves; press 3 …'

··· ··· ···

From January to April 2006, Marc tried to limit his calls to Louise. At first he maintained a boundary through calling her once a week, but as the intensity of their relationship increased he found himself using a monetary limit to contain his infatuation with her.

Over the years of using telephone sexlines Marc's pence per minute spend has decreased. When he began using the company he met Louise through, he was charged £1 a minute. But as his call frequency increased, he was exposed to more workers who told him they had a 'new' cheaper line he could ring them on. He suspected the motivation for this act of generosity was a clever manipulation to stop users like him moving to competitors' telephone lines, rather than some form of sympathy for him as a customer addicted to high cost calls.

Using a mobile phone for premium rate calls raises the per minute billing by a considerable amount. Although Marc now talks to Louise on a 35 pence a minute line, this rate applies only to calls made from a landline. In actuality he pays around 80 pence a minute each time he speaks to Louise. Marc's regular spend for his 'affair' with Louise costs him between £80 and £90 each week.

•→• •→• •→•

'… Please enter the PIN number of the operator you'd like to speak to or press the star key to return to the main menu.'

•→• •→• •→•

Marc and Louise often arrange exact times at which they will have their next call. If she picks up a client at the time they have arranged to speak, she uses all the tricks she has learned to deter callers from staying with her. The most successful rejecting is achieved from making obvious uninterested washing-up noises, turning the television on or not answering the questions asked of her while talking to a client. Simply putting the phone down on a caller is strongly discouraged, although there have been times when men with zoophilic interests telling Louise how they are 'going to get two dogs to have sex with her at the same time' have brought up uncomfortable memories she can't laugh off. Customers seem to remember girls who 'reject' and sometimes this in itself can lead to a tirade of abuse from a 'spurned' man who will go out of his way on a different day to call the operator again and let her know what a 'fucking bitch whore' she is. Louise's response to a caller who spews out his hatred of women is: *What a dumb wanker you are; you can't even see I'm having the laugh on you – I'm pissing in your face, arsehole; burn your own money dickhead.*

Louise takes great delight in 'hooking' the caller who begins by abusing her into her own web of aural sex. These men prove easy for Louise to translate into a longer-than-average caller with the concomitant result of her earning more money than she would have had they made a simple masturbatory call to her in the first place. At the end of a shift, a caller like this can even become the object of her own fantasy.

Louise is paid a flat fee for the six-hour shift she works but increment incentives are paid when she gets a caller to stay on line for forty minutes and a slightly higher rate again when a call goes over an hour. It makes Louise smile to know she is winning over an abusive man like this. It helps her to ignore the exploitation she is enduring when she stops to notice how she prostitutes her lifetime's sexual experience for a fraction of the fee the telephone network and sexline company receives for each call she conducts.

If Marc has arranged to speak to Louise and she is on a call to someone else, then Louise knows Marc is in a holding pattern entering her PIN but getting the message: 'I'm sorry, the girl you have chosen is currently on a call. Please try again later or enter another number. Press star to return to the main menu.'

Even with their joint efforts, Marc wastes several pounds each week in the process of trying to connect to her.

•◆• •◆• •◆•

Marc is lucky this time; he gets through straight away.

'I want to chat to you … properly,' Marc tells Louise. 'You know I'll give you my private mobile number.'

'I don't want to come between you and your wife, Matt; I'm just a girl on a line.'

'You are a lot more than that to me. "I bloody love you",' he mimics a stereotype of a drunk.

•◆• •◆• •◆•

There are many kinds of callers to sexlines; one group consists of men too afraid to admit they are really rather lonely and are in fact looking for a relationship. Louise never minds this sort of caller. They become regulars who return to her; they make the longer calls; they are the ones who earn her forty-minute and one-hour increments and make it easier for her to pay her mortgage. Louise thinks of these men as 'the puppies' (slightly love-sick). Their very mention of love will normally make Louise roar with laughter.

'Don't be so silly,' she will say, 'you don't love me; you love the *idea* of me. I'm just a girl on a line.'

At first, Louise thought Marc was a 'puppy' but now she is experiencing something so very real. She knows she not only loves the idea of him but something much deeper. Louise notices that even his jovial mention of love makes her feel sick. He has an enormous hold on her. She fantasizes every day about being with him. She frequently masturbates about being with him, about him dominating her and the 'switch' she attempts on him but has never quite managed since their first call together.

·•· ·•· ·•·

'I can't keep spending like this; how about a chatroom?' Marc says.

For weeks Louise has stalled Marc on this subject.

'Look I can't talk like this Matt; I've told you before I'm going to lose my job' – this is a stock phrase used by Louise whenever there is something she doesn't want to talk about – 'and the bloody company will lose its best customer.' She attempts a laugh.

Every time Louise tries to push Marc away he comes back more strongly. He is not angry with her when she deliberately misses some calls with him to get some of her own 'head space'. He understands how tricky it is for her. He says he missed her, he quotes her a poem, he tells her how if he were there with her right now he would kiss her neck, massage her tired shoulders before cupping her breasts, squeezing her nipples … Louise wants to scream at him. *Let me alone – don't you dare fucking love me!* Marc makes her *feel*. No other man has ever done this for Louise – except perhaps her therapist, and he abandoned her.

Over the course of a few more conversations, Marc finally persuades Louise to 'meet' him in an Internet chatroom. He gives her the site address to the room, then, in a different conversation, the login details and finally the passcode during a third call – just so no 'eavesdropper' can find them. His final level of security will be to change all these details again once they have made contact for the first time on the site.

Both Marc and Louise feel in danger of their developing relationship; there is a very real power differential. Marc is a company owner with a good income; he has much to lose by making poor decisions in his life. Louise is rarely solvent. She survives by being an aural prostitute and she is vulnerable. Some women do this work for kicks, some for extra cash at difficult times; yet others say they do it for a buzz or because they are lonely. Louise does it for one reason only: to make a living.

In the time Marc and Louise have been conversing he has 'taken' her away from England, ringing her while he sat by the sea watching the waves and dreaming they were making love on the sand. Even on holiday it was possible to be absent from Judy; she was easily encouraged to take a shopping trip while he stayed on the beach alone so that he could talk to Louise. In fantasy he has climbed with Louise to the tops of mountains where they have undressed and rolled in the snow, and they have kissed slowly, deeply, as if life depended on it, while looking out across the twinkling lights of Paris. Marc knows how to fuck Louise as well as make love to her; they both know the difference and neither of them is used to such intense feelings.

13 DECEMBER 2006. WELCOME TO OUR ISLAND says the opening page Marc has set up.

Enter your user name and passcode to join the chat.

Louise enters **Skippy** and the passcode Marc has given her. He has left her a message.

The Don: *from x.x.x63 joined the chat 9 hours ago*
The Don: Welcome to our tropical island Loulou. It's warm on the white sands, the sea is green, the sky is blue, the coconuts and the fruit are abundant. I've set up a rack, some chains and all the whips in the hut. Grrrrrrrrrr, mwwhhh, mwwhhh. I'll be here waiting for you, cock in hand at 19.15 when you get off work.

The Don: Mwhhh, mwwhhh – I'm going to be hot waiting for you.

The Don: *logged off 9 hours ago*

.•. .•. .•.

6.50pm Marc's head has been racing all afternoon. He has mainly refrained from using the Internet today and instead has let his excitement build up. Judy will be home at 8.30 if the train is on time so he is making decisions about what he wants to do sexually during the evening. *Shall I save a wank for online with Loulou? Knock one out now or wait until Judy gets back and have sex later? Fuck I hope Loulou has managed to get on to the Island.* Marc opens his laptop and navigates to his chatroom site.

.•. .•. .•.

WELCOME TO OUR ISLAND

Skippy: *from x.x.x111 joined the chat 5 hours ago*
Skippy: I want you to know I'm sitting here in my silk panties dripping wet for you, you lovely man. I don't know where we're going any more but I'm looking forward to it. I've never written a story for anyone before but in case you get here before me then you have something to entertain you.

Skippy: I would have called myself Loulou but then I thought that's who I pretend to be online. So I was going to call myself Louise – coz that's who I am, then I thought I'd be someone else, someone just you and me will know about. So, here I am, your Skippy. I'm glad I thought of that as you seem to be called The Don now. I told you I was good at cryptics so it only took me a couple of mins to work out yours … I take it the Don is short for Mr big boy DONKEY. You fucking better be hung like one in real life if we ever meet!!!!!! Mwwhhhhh enjoy my story!!! Bet you can't work out Skippy! LOL, LOL, LOL. Back at 19.15 or there bouts … hope the story is not too girly for you! LOL

Skippy: The story starts with you walking around in a wood with your dog. The sun is shining and it's really hot but the temperature is still cool in the woods. The sunlight is breaking through in certain places where the trees are thin. You sit down on a log to enjoy the birds singing in the tops of the trees and your dog goes sniffing about further into the woods.

Skippy: After a few moments you hear your dog barking and despite you calling him he won't come back to you. You get up from your log and go towards the sound he is making. You come to a clearing in the wood. At first you can't quite see what is in front of you as the sun is so bright, but as you look for a few moments you see a big totem pole, shaped like a cock. It's been carved out of a tree and bound tightly to it you can just make out my figure. I'm gagged and blindfolded and my skin is burning in the hot sunlight. I'm tied to the tree with my bottom sticking out towards you and there are several crazy contraptions attached to my intimate parts.

Skippy: As you walk towards me I sense your presence and can hear twigs breaking under your feet. I'm wondering who you might be and what you might do to me. The excitement makes me lose control of my bladder for a few seconds as I've been forced to drink about 2 litres of water in order to fill my bladder to bursting point. I was told by my captor that if there was any sign of fluid loss on his return I would be punished. I was told that I would be whipped in front of an audience, publicly humiliated.

Skippy: The short loss of control through the fear of your approach results in a stream of piss hitting the totem pole before it runs down to the plastic container I am standing in with my bare feet. I can feel you gazing intently at my burning rump exposed to the sun. My cheeks are taped at the outside and have thin silver chains attached to them. These in turn are nailed to two small stakes that have been hammered into the ground. The chains have just the right tension on them. They spread my arse cheeks open, displaying my moist pink flesh. You gaze even closer and see that my labia lips are …

Skippy: Part two tonight Donkey! But will you save me from my captor or *are* you my captor? God, I've made myself wet thinking about you again. I'm going to have to rub myself thinking about you now. Later mwhhh! Mmwwhhh! Mmmmwwwwhhhhh!

Skippy: *logged off 5 hours ago*

•◆• •◆• •◆•

When Marc logs in to the site he masturbates to the story Louise has written for him. It feels odd but exciting that her words are coming from the screen rather than being spoken to him. He feels excited by this new experience with Louise, excited in a way he has not been for a long time and in fact is able to ejaculate in the short time it takes him to read the story. He leaves his computer online as he takes himself to the bathroom to clean up.

•◆• •◆• •◆•

Skippy: *from x.x.x111 joined the chat at 19.17*
Skippy: Hello!

Skippy: You there?

Skippy: Bloody typical man, never one around when you want one!

Skippy: I'll just sit here typing to myself …

Skippy: It 19.21 now getting bored and have things to do like finish writing a story to some wanker I know LOL

The Don: Hello sexy!

The Don: I was here just

The Don: I

The Don: Couldn't hold myself together reading your story.

The Don: Had to do a lot of cleaning up! LOL

Skippy: Too much information LOL

The Don: This is a bit strange writing rather than talking.

Skippy: Yes, I miss your sexy voice, I always feel wet as soon as you start talking. You'll have to keep phoning me.

The Don: Well you flatter me, I don't have to hear your voice to get horny, I've just got to close my eyes and imagine you.

Skippy: Can you do photos on this site?

The Don: Why?

Skippy: So that you can send me pictures of you.

The Don: No can't do them on this site.

Skippy: Fuck! now I know you're properly ugly. Chose a site that can't do pictures!

Skippy: Ugly old Donkey, got nothing to do with your cock size then, just you a minger LOL

The Don: Well you can still have my mobile number.

Skippy: Why?

The Don: So you can see how fucking handsome I am with a MMS.

The Don: Skippy?! what kind of fucking name is that. You a bloody kangaroo? Or is it Skippy is a bush kangaroo – so you have a huge bush? LOL hairy old lady! LOL

Skippy: That would have been a good guess.

The Don: So?

Skippy: Loulou, 'skippy' to my lou! LOL

The Don: PMSL. That's bad sweetie.

Skippy: Uhh that's not very nice PMSL come and let me piss on you not you on yourself LOL

•➤• •➤• •➤•

It turns out to be very easy for Marc and Louise to converse like this. When Judy returns early having caught a different train Marc is still chatting to Louise. 'Hello love, I'll be with you in a minute,' he calls to Judy. 'I'm just finishing up some work.'

'I've brought supper in – Waitrose,' Judy responds, 'so don't be long.'

•➤• •➤• •➤•

The Don: Fuck! JJ's back, I'll have to go. Mwhhh!

Skippy: Great 11 months getting me on here now you have to go – fuck off then :-(LOL I suppose.

The Don: I'll be back here later – I can always leave a message if you are not on. I'll tell you what I'd do if I found you in the woods!!!!! And it won't just be a mmmmmwwwwwwwhhhhhhh!

Skippy: I've got to go and drop Amy off at band practice anyway so I was going anyway wanker! LOL

Skippy: That made me feel better.

The Don: LOL, LOL, LOL loves you.

Skippy: No you don't, no one loves me.

The Don: I do, I've even bought you this island.

Skippy: Ha fucking ha. If you loved me you would be with me. Now I just got a slightly bigger share in you.

The Don: Don't get like this.

Skippy: Ignore me, I'm just kidding, really.

The Don: Right I must go. Mwhhhh, you'll be in my dreams tonight sweet Loulou, Skippy, Louise whoever you are … LOL no seriously I'LL DREAM OF YOU.

Skippy: No need to SHOUT! I HEARD YOU. Mwwwhhh later. Gone now.

The Don: Mwwhhh me too.

Skippy: Mwwhh

The Don: Thought you'd gone! LOL

Skippy: Gone!

Skippy: For real this time.

Skippy: Bye, bye!

Skippy: You gone?

The Don: Yes!

The Don: PMSL

Skippy: Told you about that before!

Skippy: Gone for real this time!

The Don: Mmmhhww.

Skippy: Mmhhhw

Marc closes his laptop, cutting the connection to Louise. Then he raises the lid again for a moment and clears his browser history. He takes the seven steps to the kitchen from the chair he has been sitting in and gazes at Judy; he thinks how beautiful she looks in her work suit. He watches her body move, her buttocks straining at the fabric as she bends over to get some plates from the dishwasher.

'You had a good day then love?' she asks.

He moves over to her, 'I do love you, you know.' He puts his arms around her. He kisses her on the back of the neck and cups her breasts. Her hair smells sweet and clean, like she has just had a shower. They kiss. 'Yes, I've had a good day,' Marc says.

PART TWO

7 but my temper is spanish

27 July 2007 (session 8)

The word 'patient' can often seem an appropriate descriptor for the people I work with, since the origin of the word comes from *pati* – one who is suffering or enduring. Marc Moreau is clearly a man who is doing that.

⋅•⋅ ⋅•⋅ ⋅•⋅

'An attack could come from anywhere, at any time,' said Marc. 'She was a very unpredictable woman. I remember her saying once during a dinner party conversation that she blamed her parents for the way she behaved; my grandfather was from Paris and my grandmother, who I never knew, was from Barcelona.' Marc breaks into French for a moment, '*Je suis Français par naissance, mais ma colère est espagnole.*'

I ask him to translate his last comment for me.

'"I may have been born in France but my temper is Spanish",' he says.

'What did she mean by that?'

'She was a fiery and unpredictable person.'

'Was she always like that?'

'I can just remember a time – probably up to when I was four – when she felt safe, warm … protective … Actually an incident comes to mind. It was a wet day and we had all walked somewhere – shopping, I think. I was wearing this long grey duffel coat. It was way too big for me but she said I would grow into it; I should think myself lucky that, as the boy of the family, I got new things. My hood was up. I guess I would have been about five. I can't remember what happened but suddenly I was on the ground, flat on my back in the main road. Later I was told my coat was caught by a car we were walking past as it pulled away from the kerbside. Somehow, a thousand-to-one chance, I was dragged off the pavement and spun around 180 degrees into the road. All I can see in my mind is that there was a car stopped in front of me and my mother was going berserk. She was hammering on the window of the car shouting at the driver in French. I do believe if he hadn't driven off, she would have dragged him out of the car and beaten him to death with her bare fists.'

The room is charged. I let Marc have the space, then when it is clear he is not going to continue I say, 'So your mother defended you, she showed that she was fearful of losing you?'

'To be honest I don't know. I don't have any memories of her defending me at other times but there were plenty of occasions that she let that same temper out on me.'

I think to myself, *I wonder how much you fear that your mother might even have killed you when you were a child?* but I reply: 'You've not really said much about your mother, although I'm aware of the amount of space she seems to take up in the room here. Perhaps she's not what you want to talk about?'

'Haa!' Marc exclaims. 'As we start to move into this stuff, I realize that I probably need to talk about her more than anything. What was it you said about circles and spirals? Once we have walked around the circle of my life a few times … That's what you mean by personal social history isn't it? … You said, once we had done that, we will find the places we need to visit more deeply and then these will be the places we can visit in a spiral?'

'Something like that. The spirals are where we can travel deeper into the issues you bring. We don't just go around in circles in this work, we actually get involved in some depth work … but the more traumatic the material is, I think the more important it is that we get the timing right of when we do that work.'

'Well, I've got one fuck of a spiral here with my mother and there was never a way out of her vortex.'

•➤• •➤• •➤•

At the end of Marc's second session he asked if it was possible to do his work with me twice a week 'at least for a few weeks?' Given the power with which he was gripped by his pornographic and related sexual addictions, I felt there was a good clinical decision to be made in agreeing with his request.

In this, our eighth session together, Marc is beginning to confirm that his story fits a pattern I have found present with men who are *seriously* addicted to pornography. Although I am limited by a self-selecting clinical population and do not have research-based criteria for my observed correlations, in the vast majority of cases of serious pornography addictions I have worked with the patient has also had a pre-standing, deep-seated trauma of some nature in addition to the pornographic encapsulation that is being endured. I sit with this noticed finding in the therapy space and use it to guide me in the way I engage with a patient's story.

A tension is set up in Marc (and others like him) between an event (or set of actions) that is kept wholly or partially a secret due to its unacceptable nature and the contrary need to seek expression of the material as a form of release from it. The events that I find to be represented in men with serious pornography addictions tend to be what we would regard as various forms of trauma. Some have been experienced in childhood through physical, psychological or sexual abuse. This abuse has been enacted upon the patient by brothers, fathers, mothers, sisters, uncles, aunts, even grandparents. But the trauma may equally be found to be a major and/or catastrophic loss – for example, a mother killed in a car crash. Others, still, may be due to early and unwanted exposure to adult themes, be it as a witness to something like violence, murder, domestic violence, rape or to pornography itself.

When Marc left after his first session in June, I had ruminated on three areas: his BDSM (Bondage, Bondage and Discipline, Dominance and Submission and Sado-Masochism) fantasies with Louise; his desensitized reactions towards the Eastern European girl; and the hanging, threatening presence of his mother, Isabelle. It is now becoming clearer that Marc's relationship with his mother was an abusive one and so I am beginning to form a tentative working assumption that his relationship with his mother could be the expected trauma that accompanies his sexual acting out and addiction.

I am always careful about assumption in therapy work. The point is to listen to what is being said, not to work from one's assumptions derived from frameworks or models. However, with the emergence of deep and longstanding trauma there comes the need for a therapist to offer a particular form of protective container for a patient.

Trauma is a difficult thing to work with. There is always the danger that if you do too much of this sort of work as the therapist without sufficient self-care and self-understanding, you too can succumb to vicarious trauma. But, to my way of thinking, one of the greatest mistakes that can happen in the therapy space is the disastrous position of re-traumatizing a patient. Learning how to support or even control the patient's pace of entry and the time spent at depth is a key to trauma work, so knowing how and when to slow things down, to be the brakeman, is vital.

•◆• •◆• •◆•

'Marc, I'm looking at the clock and I see we still have thirty-five minutes of the session. If you think it might be good for you to focus on your mother, then we have enough time today to make a start.'

Marc smiles at me; he holds my gaze. It is as if he senses the containment I am offering. At moments like this patients often talk about the fact that they 'trust' me or they trust in the space. The reality is that they are, in fact, just about to begin to explore this particular part of their work. They are going to begin to test the holding function of a therapeutic relationship – a relationship that is unlike any other they have ever experienced, a relationship in which the other (the therapist) should want nothing of or from a patient, a relationship in which the flow of energy is towards the patient taking courage in his- or herself.

'She was a bitch, a wicked human being.'

Marc looks at me as if shocked that he has spoken the thought aloud or looking for confirmation that he is finally allowed to say this about his mother – without having to feign guilt. He reads my face, my non-verbal confirmation that I heard him.

'I hated her; I hated her until the day she died. I was glad when I heard her pancreas was rotting inside her, cancer transforming her body into the vile corpse I knew she had always been. I hated her every fucking time she touched me. Her griping tone, her self-centred bullying ways. Bitch! Fucking cunt! I would have loved her to come crawling to me for help in those last few days, just so I could have told her to FUCK HERSELF!' he shouts the last few words.

Not only do I hear the anger and the pain in his words, I feel the force of his emotion in my body. He is sitting on the verge of rage. His fists are clenched, his complexion reddened. I breathe more fully, slowly asking my body to both recognize Marc's broadcast but also to remain separate, to listen to itself and recognize that the impulse came from without.

Silence …

'You wanted something very different from your mother, Marc.'

Again he holds my gaze; his eyes, tears forming around the lower lids, search my face. He drops his head. 'I don't have the words for how I feel,' he says.

Silence …

Do I return to events? Silence? A comfort phrase? Reflection? Yes, a reflective phrase. I practise it: *'There are no words in the room right now.'*

Silence …

'There are no words in the room right now,' I say aloud.

Silence …

'She was like it with us all you know; we could all hear when she was hitting us. It was a big old house but I knew when she was hitting Veronique or Simone.'

'What did you do when you could hear what was happening to one of your sisters?'

'Start praying it wasn't me next. Start tidying up my room in case she came in and the state of my space became the impetus for an attack. We always had to have our rooms very tidy and clean. Mainly though, I used to put some headphones on and listen to music on my radio. I'm sure that's why I asked for headphones for my fifth or sixth birthday – so I didn't have to listen to Simone or Ronny being beaten.'

How far into the story is he going today? I'm getting used to a lot being left right to the end of the session. Marc is working out how to dump it and leave it rather than take it with him. That might be a good thing. How can I support him not having to rush it all out at the end, though? Watch the clock; bring him up ten from the end so we have some safe-space time to process.

'That must have been very frightening for you. Did the three of you help each other?'

'Mainly the girls tried to bully me. It was like in the family where father hits mother, mother hits the eldest child and so on down until the littlest child kicks the dog; guess I was the dog. But for short periods of time we could get along. I can remember one particular time the bitch was taking it out on Simone. I could hear she used the strap and the cane on her. I guess she would have been about ten years old. When I heard our bitch mother leaving Simone's room I went in to talk to my sister.'

Silence …

'Do you remember what you might have wanted to say to her?'

Silence …

'No … ummh … no. She was sobbing … and … God, it's quite difficult to say this suddenly, she was bent over her bed still, her knickers were around her ankles and her bum was bright crimson and scarred. She turned around and hissed at me – I've never seen a look on someone's face like that ever again. I got out of there as quick as I could.'

Eight minutes max before I bring him up.

'I don't want to stir too much up Marc, so let's go slowly.'

'I'm okay actually; you know I just had a real connection there. My poor old sister in that position, her arse like that; it was bruised as well as crimson …'

Silence …

'Are you making a sexual connection to that?'

'Yes … and … no. I guess … I guess I wonder what my mother was up to. Fuck! Again, this is uncomfortable but I need to say it now. When she used to beat me it was always the same: she'd pull my clothes down below the waist but quite often she would take my pants right off me and then sort of pull them, tie them around my face, over my nose.'

We mirror a synchronized shiver. Marc shakes himself as if breaking the spell of the memory.

'Have I mentioned that Ronny killed herself?'

Damn. We were doing well, just ready to rise … hard on the brakes now.

'No, that's the first time you have mentioned it.'

Good, he just looked at the clock; he might be in the present timeframe and he knows the score.

'I'm not certain it's something for now, you know. I think I get what you mean about pacing yourself. I feel really wrung out if I'm honest.'

Marc sounds fairly lucid and in touch. From my seat I can always see a clock without making the other person aware that I am monitoring where we are in the hour. 'We are getting very close to the end of the session Marc, but let's just take some time to come back up to the surface and check you're in … the right year.' I am careful how I say 'the right year'. Once, a patient thought I was making a joke with her when I said this. She was still deeply in the childhood stored within her timeless unconscious, a childhood in which no one ever took her distress seriously. Since then, I am always cautious about how I phrase the question, which seeks to confirm someone is back in the here-and-now present.

'God, it's a long time ago that now.'

'How long?'

'Ummm, twenty … no … ahh,' Marc puts his hand on his brow. His expression asks a question of me.

Simone was ten, Marc was eight, forty-one minus eight equals thirty-three years ago.

'I can't do that. God how simple! If Simone was ten, I must have been … thirty-three years ago.'

'I've asked you that, Marc, just to see where you are, to check how you're doing. When you've gone back into all that old timeless unconscious stuff you were rubbing up closely against a real trauma. Trauma makes the brain behave in some odd ways. I'll give you the scientific explanation another time – if you want it. But now we just want to let the steam out and cool back down – for want of a better phrase. How old are you?'

'Uhh?'

'How old are you now, today?'

'Oh, forty … one.'

'Can you tell me your telephone number?'

I take Marc through a few more basic questions. In processing them it allows him to emerge more fully back into the twenty-first century. I continue to talk to him but now we make light and polite conversation. I ask him where he is going after the session; if there is something he can do just for himself once he leaves; whether a nice cup of tea might be the thing to have.

'I actually have to get to the office today. I have some things to sort out with my finance director – since I couldn't do some simple maths just now I guess it's just as well I employ one for the company!'

Marc's humour is back in the room. I laugh with him and we stand up and walk to the door. We shake hands as we always do on meeting and departing. His hand is still a little clammy but he is firm in his grasp. He looks me directly in the eye as if to check the effect he might have had on me, as if to check that nothing is broken in me. 'Same time on Monday is it?'

'Yes, that's *your* session time. Twelve noon on Monday.'

'Thank you, have a nice weekend.'

'And you Marc.' *Take great care of yourself.*

8 girl in a puffa

1 June 2007

4.23pm Marc is sitting in his study. The day has gone well. He has already met the targets he set himself and has not once wandered to his Internet browser to look at pornography. He is not conscious of avoiding looking at the Internet, so there is no sense of pride in the achievement, but if he had been, he would have noticed that the seven and a half hours he has spent at work today is the longest waking period of time he has not looked at the Internet for pornography in the last twenty-three days.

As Marc flicks up his browser he is still not thinking of sex; in fact, he is looking for a new motorcycle crash helmet. However, the site he navigates to shows two pictures of a female biker in full racing leathers in the bottom left-hand corner of its home page, and in no time Marc has given up his search for a helmet and is cruising the Internet for sex scenes with female bikers in them.

◆◆◆ ◆◆◆ ◆◆◆

Marc's favourite length for sex scenes when he streams movie clips to his computer is between five and eight minutes. He finds that the longer a scene is the more he has to skip through in order to get to the material that actually turns him on. Marc also finds that when he wants to skip forward on streaming videos to get to the part of the scene he wants to watch, the bigger the file is the more likely it is to crash his computer or, equally annoyingly, the computer freezes. He can no more be bothered with 'foreplay' in a movie than he can when he is having sex with Judy. Marc often thinks how Internet porn is the sex industry's equivalent of fast food: there is no aesthetic requirement, no sense of occasion when indulging in it; simply, he thinks, *a 'fat' hit of what you want when you want it*. The twenty-three-minute movie *Biker chicks get gangbanged and squirt* currently streaming to Marc's laptop is a case in point.

Come on, come on, I'm not this patient any more. Fully signed up thirty-second culture man here you know, fucking interweb; get me to the real gang bang, the DPs or the fucking squirting – come on, fucking Internet!

Marc's screen freezes just at the point that two of the five men in the scene are about to penetrate the blonde female bikers who are spread-eagled on top of two pool tables in a seedy-looking American bar. After several different clicks of key combinations Marc is forced to quit the browser; he navigates to a different site – one of the more reliable in terms of the streamed videos it hosts or links its users to.

It has been a couple of weeks since Marc last visited this particular site and as it is updated multiple times a day with new movie clips Marc abandons his search for biker babes and begins instead to sort through the new clips that have been added since his last visit. Experience informs him that there will be something to his taste.

•◆• •◆• •◆•

The screen opens from black. A POV, close-up style, the frame is filled with a beautiful face; wisps of brunette hair fall around her cheeks. The camera is jerky and out of focus as it pulls away from her. Thirty seconds into the video, the young woman's beauty fades away into porno chic/prostitute, some sort of cropped puffa jacket, bright pink skirt and white boots. There is a poor cut in the movie and then the camera begins to pull further back. The backdrop is revealed to the spectator – the decaying housing blocks of what Marc assumes to be a former Soviet Union country. He has seen many unmemorable Eastern European women perform sexual acts in such settings.

Another cut leaves the viewer watching the young woman walking away shouting at the camera. Her body language suggests that she is very unhappy. This is not good acting; it is real life. She swings her counterfeit designer bag at a man who grabs her from the edge of the shot. The clothing set against the background and the situation is incongruous. Another poorly made edit fades in from black. The woman walks away from the camera into a passageway. As she does so there is shouting from off-screen and the woman – apparently reluctant to do so – pulls up her skirt, exposing her naked buttocks. Her underwear is absent. She looks defeated as she spins right round and finally pulls her buttock cheeks apart so that the camera can quickly focus on her intimate genital region. She spins around once more as she walks. Her vulva is completely shaven. She lets go of her cheeks and collects an anal dildo from off-screen. With disdain showing on her face she sucks it and then squats down leaning forward so that the camera can film her inserting the butt plug into her anus. The look of humiliation on the female's face only serves to make Marc stiffer as he masturbates to the video. In his mind he is with Louise, imagining her mock indignation at having her anus filled in such a way.

The woman's clean bright clothes shine out in the dimly lit passageway. The pink is almost fluorescent. Once she has fully inserted the dildo she turns and looks at the camera. Her smile is dead. She is looking off-camera for her cues of what to do next. Marc does not notice how young looking this 'performer' is. In his mind she is Louise. In his mind, when he is aroused, a film makes things consensual and what he is seeing is the acting out of fantasy. Marc is not conscious of breaking his own rule about teen sex videos but the reality is that he is looking at a teenager, a girl without experience of life. Watching her pose and move and penetrate herself is like watching a trained animal posed by its handlers in order to make the series of learned moves look like conscious actions. This is not consensual sexual activity.

The girl begins to walk forward again still with the plug inserted in her anus. A split second later two young boys cycle past her; they are about eight years old.

The camera follows the girl across a courtyard and into a stairwell. A few steps inside, the woman drops to her knees. A penis is thrust into her mouth, rapidly becoming erect. She deep throats it on the doorstep to one of the flats. She slurps, gurgles, gags and leaks spittle and bile from the sides of her mouth. Her eyes water. A hand pulls the butt plug from her anus and she is forced to perform an ATM (arse to mouth) by exchanging the penis for the plug. The movie clip is edited once more. Any unaroused viewer would quickly recognize that the girl has been crying, that something happened between the on-screen edits. The spittle continues to roll out of her mouth as she sucks on the plug. After a few seconds she removes the dildo and holds her mouth open. Her tongue slowly pokes out of her mouth as the penis is masturbated inside her orifice; she is being made to look like a gargoyle. Finally the penis ejaculates onto her tongue and further spasms shoot the semen into the back of her throat. She gags slightly before bringing the ejaculate to the front of her mouth for the camera and then with a poke to the ribs she swallows it. As she swallows, her pained face does not betray her distaste and she gags as the sperm begins its descent of her alimentary canal.

Marc's masturbation is reaching its crescendo; he is barely seeing the images on screen.

A disembodied hand at the edge of the shot reinserts the plug into the female's anus and she continues her ascent of the decaying concrete staircase. A storey or so higher, outside the entrance to another flat, she leans forward onto the cold grey wall and removes the anal dildo once more. She performs another ATM with it. She looks like a baby would, sucking a dummy. The camera closes in to focus on her rump as an erect penis enters her anus and roughly penetrates her. The buggering she receives is mercifully short; the disconnected penis ejaculates inside of her. She holds her buttock cheeks open for the camera and Marc witnesses the anal cream pie that was promised in the title of the video. The sperm is collected in a shot glass before the hand brings it in front of her mouth and she is forced to swallow the ejaculate from the glass.

The close of the movie clip shows the door of the flat opening and a stern middle-aged man with greying hair drags the girl into the flat; he pushes her and slaps her. The camera follows and as she is bundled into a bedroom; the camera shows a close-up of the 'actress' in what looks like a school class photograph. The photograph is recent and clearly implies that the girl whose 'rape' has been shown as entertainment to the rest of the world is at best only just above the legal age of consent.

Marc closes his laptop; as he sits quietly reflecting on what he has just orgasmed to, he feels a little ashamed of himself having noticed by the end of the video the reality of it. Momentarily he remembers the pathos he had once felt for the character of Lilya in Lukas Moodysson's 2002 film *Lilya 4-Ever*. The film tells the story of sixteen year-old Lilya who, in her naïve wish for a better life in Western Europe, is trafficked out of a former Soviet republic to Sweden only to be enslaved, prostituted, abused and multiply raped. In one particularly harrowing scene it is implied that she is anally raped while role-playing a customer's daughter.

Marc had just ejaculated as he had watched the girl in the puffa jacket empty her anus of sperm. *I've seen videos like this before,* he thinks. He never gives the women in them a second thought, but he remembers Lilya still after five years. He remembers that Lilya had been based on the real-life story of Danguole Rasalaite, a Lithuanian girl who was trafficked into Malmö, Sweden, as a sex worker and who committed suicide just like Lilya.

While Marc sits, his disquiet does not fade to relief. He comes to realize that he has *not* seen other videos like this one. Always in the past he has been able to see that the videos have been acted out – some have been very realistic but there would always be a 'tell' somewhere. While he sits in his ergonomic designer home office chair listening to his computer quietly spin down to silence, he hopes he will awaken from the nightmare feeling that is growing inside of him – but he knows he is not sleeping. Had he just been masturbating to a video of abuse? Of real abuse, not simulated? Had he just seen a woman raped? Had he in fact just seen a *girl* raped? Had he just seen a *child* raped? His head is hot, he feels dirty, he feels sick, he is sweating; if he has just seen a child being forced to have sex and he had just achieved an orgasm as the seminal fluid of the man dripped from the abused anus, *What in the fuck have I become?* he shouts inside his head.

Marc runs to the bathroom. He is sick, not just physically but sick to his core, sick with himself, with society, with what he is doing – has done to himself. He is genuinely fearful. Not only fearful of what he has seen or that he might in some way be seen as being the same as the men who had just done this to a child, but also fearful that the most awful outcome of using pornography had just found him and that it was too late, that it was only after the event he had been able to see that what he had just witnessed was the awful abuse of a child or a teenager little more than a child. This is something that will now always be in his head. Life, mankind, society, Marc thinks, is utterly rotten and he feels himself to be at its very centre. His mind continues to race and ask questions. Was the man who opened the flat door the actress's father? Can life really be so bad that a man would use his own daughter in a film like the one he had seen? Every awful rape and abuse case he has ever heard of is in his mind.

Marc is shaking, as if going into shock. His knees buckle, he is clammy, pale, his heart is racing. He lies down on the bathroom floor; he wishes himself dead at that moment. The most worthless moment of his entire life.

᛫᛭᛫ ᛫᛭᛫ ᛫᛭᛫

5.56pm Marc is only unconscious for a second or two. As he stirs he thinks about Louise and all the ways they have been together and yet never touched, never hugged, never kissed. The worthlessness that has engulfed him makes him react in a particular way. Marc wants to be close, as close as he can be, to the person who makes him feel the greatest sense of life within himself. Being able to watch and remain aroused by the video of the abused girl proves the psychological danger he is in.

The stories and fantasies that Louise uses with Marc have always been based on her own abuse. Although Marc knows this he does not acknowledge it. When Louise cries on the phone to him at unhappy moments he plays the good father, and yet another day he rapes her, he abuses her – because she asks for it. The abuse he suffered himself, as a child, becomes a priming impetus for his attacks on Louise, somehow rounding the circle in his mind.

Despite Marc's heavy use of pornography he has not previously experienced a sudden pornographic trauma. He has in fact unknowingly become accustomed, desensitized to videos of abuse, but the video of the Eastern European girl has altered this and it has been the final step in breaking Marc, at least temporarily. For some time he will be incapable of maintaining appropriate, protective boundaries of his own.

In his trauma state, Marc feels that things are suddenly clear and he is quite certain what he should do.

Opening his browser once more, he types the address for the Island and logs in to the site.

The Don: *from x.x.x63 joined the chat*
The Don: Loulou, stuff in a mess in my head. Didn't want to call you on your mobile as I know you working right now. Let's meet next week when you have time off. JJ's in NY for the week so we can meet pretty much any place. God I'm really fucked up – I'll phone you later in the week for a bit of a chat but I think I just need to see you. You've been right that's all I'm saying …

The Don: I'll check back here later and see what you say – fuck, I'm such a fool.

The Don: Fuck this website, don't take the above the wrong way, I don't mean a fool to meet you, I mean what I do.

The Don: gone at 18.14 Mwwwhhh.

Later in the evening Marc goes back online to see if Louise has responded to him.

Skippy: *x.x.x111 joined the chat 1 hour ago*
Skippy: Your message seems a little confused Matt. Do you really want to meet with me?

Skippy: I can only say that I'd love to but am a little scared that you'll leave me hanging around like a spare part. If you are not certain don't play with me. I want to meet you, I want you to fuck me, take me in all the ways I've described in all our chats. If you just fancy the idea of me but don't want to go through with it, that's fine, we can just be friends. But we can't go through this process more than once. We set a date you need to be there. If not then pull out now. You can then never have me, I can never have you but we can still hang around here and the phones for a while.

Skippy: NO YOU KNOW WHAT – fucking love me or leave Matt.

Skippy: gone at 19.22 – I'll be back in an hour to see if we are meeting.

When Marc logs back in he reads what Louise has written to him.

The Don: *x.x.x63 joined the chat 4 mins ago*
The Don: Staying on here 'til you come back on.

The Don: I'm working on my laptop so you are in the corner of the screen! Don't leave if I miss you for a moment or two.

The Don: 20.40 you having a long hour. I've read your message and I want us to meet.

The Don: Still here!

Skippy: *x.x.x111 joined the conversation*
Skippy: Hello tosser! LOL

Skippy: Reading the shite you write when I'm not here are you?

Skippy: Try looking in the corner of your screen!!!

Marc placed his sex SIM in his mobile while he was waiting for Louise to come online. He has walked away to the kitchen to pour some wine when the phone rings.

'Hello big boy – you blind as well as ugly,' says Louise.

'Sorry sweetie, forgot to mention the bottle-bottom glasses I wear!' He laughs out loud.

'Well, you finally made up your mind what you are doing then.'

'Yes,' Marc says. 'It's been a strange day, I just realized I had nothing to lose.' There is a pause. 'I don't mean it like that.'

'Glad to hear it.'

'I just want to be with you, I want to feel your skin under my touch, I want to kiss your lips, Lou.'

Louise purrs at Marc, 'When, Matt, when we meeting?'

'JJ's away in New York next Monday for the week – I can move my work around for you, as you like.'

'I'll take you from Monday to Friday then!' Louise laughs. Marc is almost crying on the other end of the phone; he blows her a kiss to disguise his voice. 'Monday, Matt. Let's meet, fuck, have sex, make love on Monday – I'm wet just thinking about it. My pussy will probably need a plaster on it by the time we meet because of over-use thinking about what you might do to it. Where's JJ? Thought she was home tonight?'

'Funny you should mention her; I can just see her coming onto the drive now.'

'Bye, bye my donkey, sweet dreams – sweet ass.'

'Mwhh, catch up for details tomorrow.'

9 in front of the mirror

9.46am It's hot sitting in the window of the café even though it is still quite early morning. Louise has packed a bag of clothes that she feels will be right for an overnight stay in a hotel. She has also packed her favourite sex toys and devices in order that everything would be to hand. On Saturday morning she visited her local chemist and bought a large box of Durex and some K-Y Jelly. She placed the jelly in a separate bag with a home enema kit.

.•. .•. .•.

Louise scans the driver of each car as it pulls into the car park. Since their first sexline conversation when Marc gave Louise his made-up self-description he has always refused to tell her what he looks like and this has been an unbearable tease for her. When they began to use their private mobile phones to contact each other it was only a couple of days before Louise sent Marc a picture of herself. The image she sent showed her sitting at her dressing table brushing her long brunette hair. Amy took the photo of her wearing a flimsy black satin top for a new online dating entry; 'It shows how beautiful you still look mum,' she said.

When Marc received the picture of Louise as part of a text message he phoned her almost immediately. 'My God Loulou, I think you look so fucking beautiful, I want you now you hot bitch!' (When Marc and Louise began to arrange the details for their meeting he asked her if she still has the satin top. She said she does and that she would put it in her bag for when they meet.) Louise assumed that, in return, Marc would send her a picture showing what he looks like, too, but he did not. Over the next few days he sent her a close-up of an eye, his ear, even the head of his penis as it ejaculated with the attached message:

Thinking of you when this happened!
Mwh Matt xxx

On Saturday, as they finalized their arrangements for their rendez-vous, she mentioned that she still doesn't know how she will recognize him. 'Are you going to send me a picture of your face before it's too late for me to run away,' she said rather sarcastically.

'Loulou, I know what you look like – beautiful. I won't miss you and I don't think you'll miss me. Put all the pieces together and I'm certain you'll spot me the second I drive into the car park; you poor girl, you'll understand. God, I'm an arrogant shit aren't I?'

▪▸▪ ▪▸▪ ▪▸▪

Louise sips her coffee, running everything through in her mind. A big new Mercedes parks outside. She makes the connection to Marc's love of cars. The man who gets out of the vehicle is in his forties, a little short and to be honest carrying too much weight. He walks into the café. Louise practises her smile. She is disappointed. The man she thinks of as her Matt has much more style than the man who has just walked in. He looks around the room. Louise is not certain whether to rise and greet him or raise the newspaper in front of her face. *Perhaps if he had prepared me for what he looked like with a photo I could feel warm right now*. But another thought is already going around her mind: once more she will have to give her body over tonight to a fat, middle-aged man who wants to take from her. She already knows how it will feel. When he is inside her it will be like when they held her in front of the mirror and buggered her, raped her, made her fellate all her father's 'friends'. How she still hates those men. How she now feels so shamed that she dared to imagine something different from her Matt. *I knew it when he didn't send me the photo.*

'Jack! Over here mate,' a voice calls from the other side of the busy café. The portly man raises his hand and walks to meet his business contacts.

Thank fuck for that. I thought I'd cry if he touched me, if I had to smile at his mug.

Louise looks around the café. She is planning an escape route if she needs it. All the positive anticipation has been lost. She looks at her watch; it is 9.54am. Marc is nine minutes late now. *Will he really come after all? Can't I just have a shining knight even for one day? God! You have punished me so long and for what? I know he's a married man – but I'm not making him do this. Anyway, Judy doesn't love him, not like I do; if she did she would spend more time with him. Listen to me, talking to a god I don't think exists about a man I've never met and who has probably left me sitting in a café in Sussex looking like a stupid bitch. If I think about it, he's hardly told me any- thing about himself really. I know what he* feels *like but I don't know what he* looks *like, what he does for a job. Sure, I know he had a shite family like me. Oh fuck! What am I doing here – I've got to get out!*

At the same moment as Louise is thinking about her escape, Marc drives into the car park. Louise hardly hears the note of the V8 Jaguar XK8R – Marc's £70,000-plus toy. However, she does see a very hand- some man step out of the Jag. *Could it be him?* Her guts churn, her head goes light, she feels spaced, trapped, excited, shameful, ugly, sad.

Marc pushes open the door. *I should have texted her, let her know that I was caught in traffic, made her feel safe. Fuck what am I doing? You know you want this really; Lou understands you.* He does not pause when he comes through the door; he scans as he walks further into the café. *What if that was a picture of someone other than her or it was taken fifteen years ago before she went to seed … God! No, there she is!*

Marc is striding towards Louise.

It's him; it really fucking is him. Louise has tears in her eyes.

'Loulou, at last,' Marc touches her cheek. *It's so warm; she is so pretty to me.*

'Matt,' is all Louise can manage. They kiss and then sit down next to each other in the booth. Marc takes her right hand in his left and they sit in silence for a few moments.

'Well, here I am at last; bet you thought I wasn't coming! I knew I should have texted you … sorry.'

Louise is snuggling up to Marc's shoulders. 'Youz here – what do we do now?'

'I booked the hotel room for last night as well as today.'

'Uhh?' she says.

'I booked it for last night so that we didn't have to wait 'til 3pm to check in today. We can go straight there now, if you'd like to. It's only a few minutes away really. You okay to leave your car here?'

Louise's car is the thirteen year-old rusting Fiesta parked three spaces from Marc's gleaming Jaguar. Two out of four wheel trims on her vehicle are missing. She calls it her 'ashtray (almost) on wheels'. Louise would like Marc not to see what she drove to meet him in – his presence is very exact. The cloth of his shirt is fine and moves around him perfectly. His trousers are exquisitely cut, fitting him like he was born wearing them. 'I've just got a couple of bags,' she says.

⫸⫷ ⫸⫷ ⫸⫷

Marc drives fast. Louise is not certain if he is trying to impress her or if he always drives like this. Either way, she enjoys the ride, the leather sports seats hugging her figure as the car twists through the B road route to the country house hotel.

When they arrive, Louise is speechless. This is a different life to the one she is used to. *How much money must you have to bring us here? You even wasted a night's money on this place just so we could have the room this morning. God! You are making a monkey out of me.* Louise stands quietly to the side of Marc and lets him book them in. They have a luxury suite.

From the small lobby space the suite opens into large sitting and bedroom spaces, Louise paces the main room. *Yes, bigger than the whole of my downstairs.* The room is a fusion of modern and classical styles with a four-poster bed, bathed in opulent colours. On the table in front of the window is a bowl of fruit and by the side of the bed some newly placed hand-made chocolates and fresh cut flowers. The bathroom has a wet room area and in the middle a beautiful rolltop bath. Marc smiles at Louise, 'Good enough for you?'

'God, it's like I'm in a bad romance novel, except it's also just like I imagined it would be with you, but you are better looking and fuck you must be a lot richer than I thought.'

'It's been a good couple of years for the company; rich I'm not.'

'Won't Judy want to know where all this money has gone?'

'I'm not poor either! Judy earns almost as much as I do and we keep our own "winnings". You and I can have whatever we want while we're here, everything is cash – so no nasty mistakes to be found out with; the hotel is very discreet, they can tell we're not married.'

'Really? Of course they can. It's just like me on the lines I suppose; I can tell what men are looking for before they ask for it. It's just this is not much like my life.'

'Well enjoy it then while it's here.'

'Matt are you …'

Marc interrupts Louise, 'Look, I've got to get this out before we move on: I'm not Matt, I'm Marc – with a "c".'

Louise is taken aback. His name at least, she thought, was his; even if she had nothing else of him, she thought she had his name. 'Why did you lie to me?'

He shrugs his shoulders, 'Don't ask me. But now I'm correcting it, correcting it before we start things here.'

'Don't be a prick! Start things! What the fuck are you talking about? What's the last year and a half been if it's not starting things? – you prick, you fucking prick!'

Louise is incandescent with rage. Marc recoils; another woman is attacking him. He moves towards her and she starts to hit out at him. Although his six-foot one-inch frame could so easily restrain her, he does nothing to prevent a volley of slaps hitting him. A masochistic numbness cloaks him as Louise begins to punch him. He deserves this, he thinks; Louise is his mother, then his big sisters, then Judy railing at him. Louise's rage burns for a full twenty minutes. At the end of it she is slumped in the middle of the beautiful room. Her smudged mascara makes her look like a heroin chic catwalk model. Her hair is dishevelled, her sleeves pushed up, her skirt twisted around her, almost back to front. Marc is looking at her, head slumped down to meet her gaze. As she sobs she finally looks up to meet his eyes, his beautiful sparkling green eyes. 'Are you … Are we finished now?' he whispers to her.

Louise is ashamed of herself. 'Marc? That seems so odd to say out loud, to really know your name. Marc what?'

'Marc Moreau.'

'A French name?'

'Yes. I think I told you my father was an academic; he brought my mother to England when he'd finished his PhD. All true Loulou, just my name was missing. I never lied to you; I just didn't give you all the details. I'd rather hold back things than lie to you.'

'You beautiful man. Marc with a "c".' Louise chokes on her words.

'I'm here, me, Marc,' he says.

Louise blows him a kiss.

'I'll tell you one thing Loulou, there's no way the staff could think we're not married after that row.'

Marc's humour shines through. *How does he manage this?* Louise thinks. She moves forward to Marc and kisses him on the lips. 'I'm sorry, so sorry,' she says.

'Me too, sorry for everything that ever happened to you Lou.'

'The two of us,' Louise says, 'sorry for everything that ever happened?'

Neither quite knows what the other means and yet they are truly meeting in this moment. Louise stands up, undoes her skirt and lets it fall to the floor. Marc unbuttons his shirt, takes it off and drops it on her skirt. Louise removes her top. Marc takes off his trousers as if in response. He is beginning to stiffen with the erotic charge in the room.

'This is not how I meant it to be, not how I've dreamed of it for the last year or more,' Louise says.

'Things have a habit of being like this in my life sweetie.'

Louise takes herself to the bed. 'We have the four-poster! Now we've done it in one of these before haven't we?'

'Our third call wasn't it?' Marc replies. They sit on the bed. He unhooks her bra, slides her briefs down her legs and removes them over her feet. He gently rolls Louise over onto her side and positions himself so that he can spoon with her. He kisses the back of her neck as his penis becomes fully erect. He nestles its head against her labia, getting ready to enter her.

'I have Durex,' she says.

'When did you last have sex, Lou?'

'Three years ago, why?'

'Well you're not going to give me anything, and I've not slept with anyone else since I got married, so why bother?' He pushes himself inside her with some force.

'I'm not on the pill you jerk.'

'I won't cum in your pussy then.' Marc enjoys the gentleness with which he has taken control of her, made her submit to his wishes, his desire.

'But I want you to come inside me Matt … Marc.'

'Then I'll fuck you up the arse – I'll empty my seed in your rectum.' These words excite them both.

Louise is speaking quickly; there is real excitement and anxiety in sex for her. 'But you will have to use a Durex in my arse; it's the only "safe" way with me unless I've had an enema. I don't want you to get s …'

Marc places his hand over Louise's mouth. 'Shhhh, go with me, I'm in control now.'

Marc continues to plough into Louise. For an hour they have sexual intercourse in many different positions. The pleasure is enormous for both of them until they find themselves in front of the full-length dressing mirror.

·❖· ·❖· ·❖·

Louise has told Marc about how she had been abused until the onset of her menarche in her early teens. They have even descended into a dark space where their joint abuses have overlapped, where each has played the abuser for the other, sometimes to a simple triumph, sometimes to a complex orgasm that has not been understood by either party.

•←• •←• •←•

Marc can see his naked torso above the body of his lover; the mirror is reflecting the reality back to them. Louise, on her knees on the floor, passes Marc a condom and the tube of lubricant gel. She then places a hand on each of her buttock cheeks and spreads them wide open looking at Marc in the mirror. It is a re-creation of abuse – childhood abuse and the abuse she suffered with her second husband. It is the way Louise thinks she must give herself to Marc. It is the way that she has gone on punishing herself even after she escaped her father, his friends and her second husband. It is the compound of things she has come to expect. In Marc's mind, suddenly he is with the girl in the cropped puffa jacket and pink skirt. He looks down at Louise's rump, her spread cheeks, her vulnerable openings and he begins to cry. His penis rapidly becomes flaccid. Louise lets go of her cheeks; she surges forward and lies on her stomach. Marc follows her. She does not speak to him. They simply lie on the floor; Marc holds Louise tightly.

•←• •←• •←•

Lunch is a time for recovery. Louise has the fagottini stuffed with organic carrots, greens and ricotta cheese, followed by carpaccio of tuna and wild sea bass sandwiched with wasabi. Marc takes the celery shoots and Gruyère gougère followed by baked bream with Provençale vegetables. While he thinks the food is only a little better than average, Louise has never had such a grand meal – nor spent so much. For her, spaghetti bolognaise and a bottle of Peroni would have been just fine. She finds the wine bill horrific, but she can finally understand how it is that Marc could sustain the phone bills he used to run up with her when they spoke on the chatline. In her head she is trying to calculate exactly how many hours' work she would have to do to pay for this meal. She gives up when she sees that it is far in excess of a day and a half.

10 a respectable woman

WELCOME TO OUR ISLAND

Skippy: *from x.x.x111 joined the chat 6 hours ago*
Skippy: Hello my love. I'm all wet waiting for tomorrow to come around or should that be cum around. LOL. Can't believe it's been almost 3 months since we first met. Can't wait to find out what you've planned. And believe me you won't be able to hold out long on what I've got planned for you Donkey boy! LOL LOL LOL mmwwhhh

Skippy: I woke up last night from the most wicked dream about you. You had me on all fours. You were the photographer on a pornography shoot and you were making me perform in various acts that I hadn't wanted to do. I was being taken by two beautiful hunks, they were spit-roasting me, then they DP'ed me before giving me a long hard anal fuck – just like you always want to give me when we talk on the phone. I could only let them do it to me because all the time I was looking straight into your lens, looking at your handsome features. I was imagining you whipping my arse, beating me as a punishment for my whore-like behaviours. Then I woke up just as the fun was about to start! LOL I really can't wait to know what you have planned for us this weekend, really intriguing. It's going on a surprise date I guess.

Skippy: You won't turn into a mad man though will you? I don't want to get cut up and put in the boot you know!! I don't mind if you enslave me with your charms and make me work for you by having sex with handsome men though. Then chaining me, beating me like 'O', like in my dreams LOL.

Skippy: I don't have time to write you a fantasy today but I printed that one out you wrote me yesterday about Paris. I'd love to do that for you. I'd love to be able to expose myself just like you wrote. It made me no better than a cheap street whore but I wanted to do it for you, just like that. Oooooooohhhhhhhhhhhh la la. LOL

Skippy: I keep on reading myself bits of it – especially the bit where you tie me up and use the syringe. Made me gush you know. About tomoz, I'm telling myself I shouldn't get my hopes up coz I know we are not going to Paris otherwise you'd have asked me to check my passport. Boooo hisssssss. Mr Mean Donkey – LOL only joking. The prize is getting to lie next to you. To have you penetrate me in all my holes, strip me bare. God I've got to stop writing this. I'm working myself up into a state again. Mwwhhhh

Skippy: I'll be back here later for the directions you promised. They better not be 'stand in the corner with your knickers at half-mast' again. But that did make me laugh Marc, I felt like doing it for real, on my own, because you had COMMANDED me to. Oooohhhhh I'm going to need some huge orgasms this weekend and many of them. I'm going to pack the drafting tube with my best cane and crop so you can beat, mark me and make me cum just like we have talked about.

Skippy: I'll send you a text if you've not put the directions up by 6 just in case your Internets down or sumut?! Why do I still worry you'll let me down? Worry, worry. Mwwhhh

Skippy: *logged off 6 hours ago*

The Don: *from x.x.x63 joined the chat 4 hours ago*
The Don: Follow these instructions to the letter.

The Don: Before you leave your house, I want you to masturbate yourself but DO NOT allow yourself to orgasm. When you first feel yourself begin to reach a climax get up from your bed and put the black underwear on that I gave you when we met in June. I also want you to wear a black skirt and your black satin top. Although you may drive in any footwear you want, by the time we meet you must have already changed into high heels.

The Don: You should drive up to Cambridge on the M11. At the first turnoff marked for Cambridge South (A1309) indicate and then drive to the roundabout. Take the third exit marked to Cambridge Park and Ride. Drive along the road until you come to a Waitrose on your LH side. Take the next turning (Maris Lane) marked to Grantchester. Follow the road through to Grantchester. Drive across the river and continue along the road until you pass the Green Man on your RH side and then the Rupert Brooke also on your RH side. Follow the road on again (Broadway) until you come to a row of Victorian houses on your LH side (there is a pub called the Blue Ball Inn). Park up as far along that road as you can find a space. Get out of the car and be waiting at the rear of your vehicle for 3.30pm. Your carriage will await you and will transport you to where you are to spend the weekend in the company of yours truly. Madame, any deviation from this set of directions will result in a quite severe punishment. You have been warned.

The Don: God, I've made myself hot as well now – Perhaps I'll make tomorrow into our own 'Story of O'. LOL. Mwwhhh

The Don: btw, it's ok, I won't blindfold you or stick you in the boot – much as you deserve it just for the insult you threw in expecting me to let you down. Grrrrrrr.

The Don: *logged off 4 hours ago*

Skippy: *from x.x.x111 joined the chat 2 hours ago*
Skippy: You have me panting here not knowing what we are going to be up to. Have this fantasy you are going to take me to your house and tie me up for the weekend, spank me, beat me, whip me before you torture my poor pussy and my delicate rear entrance. Stupid I

know … but I'm on the edge of passing out with anticipation Marc. Your reference to O just makes it worse; I can imagine you making me undress in your beautiful car like O had to in the taxi. You'd be inspecting my panties as you drove and folding them up and gagging me with them. ohhhhhhhh

Skippy: I'm going to have to work all tonight so I'm not going to check back in until tomoz. I'll have a good kip when I finish at 7 and then I'll be at Grantchester at 3.30 – traffic permitting! Mwhhhh dream of me when sleep time comes. I'm worth it LOL. btw, I'll follow your rules, every one of them. I really will let you inspect my panties when I arrive in case you need the evidence that I've been a good girl and got myself hot and bothered before I left home.

Skippy: *logged off 2 hours ago*

•◆• •◆• •◆•

2.47pm Marc is on his mobile to Judy, 'Have a safe flight. I'll see you when you get back on Tuesday.'

'I still can't believe I've actually got to do a sit-down with them on a Friday *and* a bloody Monday. They never think about the fact there's a fucking weekend in the middle.'

'You said all this last night, JJ. I'm starting to think you're actually feeling guilty for leaving me all alone, again. I know you just want to go shopping in Milan for the weekend, really.'

'Well, I do still have a few things to get for Switzerland and that's only two weeks away. I'm looking forward to our holiday, aren't you? Mwhh. Got to go now; first call for my flight and I've still got to pick up something to read … Bye.'

'Oh … JJ, I forgot to say I'm going to head up to Norfolk tomorrow for the weekend. A family just pulled out of their stay for this week so I thought I'd go up and spend the weekend there as you are away.'

'Yes, good idea, enjoy your weekend – don't do anything I wouldn't! Mwhh.'

'Safe trip. Mwhh.'

The phone goes dead. Marc thinks of Judy rushing to WHSmith to pick up some trash, high-volume-selling chick lit for the five days she is about to spend in Milan. For a moment he has a conscious concern for Judy as he notices how easy it was for him to lie to her. It was only when he finally told her, at the end of their conversation, about the family cancelling their booking that he had confirmed in his own mind that he *wanted* to take Louise to his Norfolk holiday home. In fact, little more than a week ago he had gone to great trouble to book a hotel room for his weekend-long liaison.

Marc and Judy bought their holiday home to spend winter week-ends in. It is there that they have been each of the last eight Christmas holidays. Marc remembers the feeling he had the first time he lit the fire in the house after the renovation, how he and Judy had spread themselves out in front of it and kissed like they had done when they were first in love with each other. That night, Judy had undressed him and herself as they lay on the rug. She had taken his penis in her hand and with a gentle tug persuaded him to be led by it up the stairs and into the master bedroom.

The truth is, the family had cancelled their booking for the property a week ago – the day after Marc had found out Judy was off to Italy. It is Marc who deals with the letting agent and he had told them not to bother filling the gap, as he would use it himself. He now wonders what it might mean that he wants to take Louise to his and Judy's bolthole. He thinks about how he will recount this whole episode in his therapy space.

Marc picks up the phone once more and dials; a hotel reception-ist answers. After some negotiation, Marc agrees a cancellation fee for the Friday night and, given the circumstances of the cancellation, rolls over the advance payment for another stay, as long as it's within three months. *My wife's been taken ill? She's in hospital? What in the fuck am I up to? This has got to stop, Moreau. No messing, I do need the therapy. God, I want her though – what in the fuck am I like!?* He reclines in his chair; almost everything is in place now for tomor-row's tryst. As he begins to imagine how their time together will play out he turns to his laptop. It is 3.32pm and he has to return to the office by 4.30pm. With the browser open he types in the address of his favourite porn hub. He clicks his cursor on the search box in the top right-hand corner of the site and keys in 'speculum play'. Marc is looking for a particular video he remembers. He has been fantasizing about enacting it with Louise. The movie clip involved extracting sperm from the woman's vagina and sucking it up in a syringe before opening her vagina with a speculum, then penetrating her cervix with the syringe and squirting the contents back inside her. *Come on, I know it's here; I'm fucking desperate to come, and quickly.*

••• ••• •••

After finishing his work yesterday, Marc spent almost the whole evening masturbating to more and more extreme online pornography. Marc is in a period of being particularly turned on by gynaecological pornography, the impetus coming from a recent mobile call with Louise. Masturbating together, Marc had become very aroused when she kept asking him to insert objects into her vagina and, most particularly, when she demanded: 'Look into my pee hole; find it, stretch it open and insert the thin end of my make-up brush into it; do it *now*!'

Despite intuiting that this was a re-enactment of some scene from Louise's own story of childhood sexual abuse, Marc found the whole conversation extremely stimulating. For Marc, the whole gyno-porn area is a crossover from his BDSM interests. He enjoys the restraint placed on the women in the movie clips he has watched and he enjoys a sub-genre that is, for the most part, shot as faceless: extreme close-ups of the women's genitalia being penetrated with medical equipment. The women are categorized in Marc's mind as extreme objects that consent to being tormented, used, abused, played with and even sometimes allowed to show apparent or real pleasure from the things enacted on them. Marc has had desires to 'play' in this area before. During the previous summer he spent several weeks surfing for movies of men having their penises penetrated by urethral sounds and he even began to enter his own urethra while simultaneously inserting a butt plug into his anus.

••• ••• •••

Marc's therapy session this lunchtime had become bogged down in defence of the activities he has planned for the weekend ahead. He had already cancelled his Monday session. The desire to go through with his meeting with Louise is as yet far greater than his desire to repair himself. He wants the love and attention he thinks Louise can give to him. He wants to be able to play with his fantasies with her in the most private of settings.

Marc has a sense of guilt and extreme disappointment in himself as he leaves his session. He knows he has not only been lying to a person who would not judge him for his actions but perhaps, more importantly, to himself as well. He thinks about how he has just wasted something in a rather spectacular and yet still totally private fashion. There is a familiar sense of worthlessness that once more pervades him.

Marc sits in his car, reflecting on the session. He grips the steering wheel with angry hands – angry at himself. *I am never doing that again. What would I have lost by talking about what I'm about to do. It's not like I'm going to be told I can't do it. I couldn't be told I can't have the weekend with Lou. Fuck, I might even have been able to work out something about this whole fucked-up mess. What is the fucking point in pretending I want to stop being like this if I'm lying to myself? I'm such a wanker!*

Marc remains in this low frame of mind as he returns to his business premises. He sits in the office with the life of his company moving around him. He holds his mobile telephone in his hand. He thinks of phoning Louise. He imagines saying to her: *I'm really sorry, I think I must have eaten something that was off yesterday evening. I've been up all night with the Tijuana trots and I didn't want to phone you earlier as I thought it would have cleared up by now, but it hasn't.*

He looks at his watch. 2.30pm. *She is well on her journey. How could I let her down like that?* As he imagines her driving to Cambridge he sees the smile on her face. He feels the excitement she imbues in her chatroom messages. His pulse rises, his guts churn and a conditioned response emerges. It is like switching off one part of his brain and switching on another. He thinks about Louise, *her beautiful face driving to see me; she's like a young woman, not a forty-something. God her body's fantastic, I'm going to fuck that beautiful woman so many times this weekend.*

·•· ·•· ·•·

Marc enters Grantchester from the opposite direction to Louise and sees her standing behind her car looking around. She is in the black satin blouse he told her to wear – he thinks that it is undone one button too many for any respectable female. He thinks her skirt is an inch or so too short for a respectable woman and her shoes have heels that make it look as if she is almost standing on tiptoes. He aches at the idea that she is uncomfortable and feeling exposed. *Fuck, what more could a man want from a woman for the weekend?*

Marc has pulled his car alongside hers on the narrow street. A bus is waiting to proceed but Marc is blocking the way. 'There you are sweetie, I didn't know if you'd be walking or driving to meet me. I've felt like such a tart standing in the road looking around dressed like this.'

'Good. Have you got your bags?'

'Check!'

With a laugh in his voice Marc says, 'What are you waiting for then – I'm not getting out to get them for you, you old tart! There's a fucking bus waiting to get down here you know.'

Louise totters around the car on her high heels. She pushes her bag and drafting tube into the boot of the Jag and flings herself unceremoniously into the passenger side of the car. Almost before she has gained balance in the seat Marc is accelerating towards the bus at speed.

'Woooooow … Aahhh …' Louise squeals with excitement.

11 do you know bettie page?

'It was still dark when I opened my eyes,' says Marc. 'I think it was about 3 o'clock. I was just aware of this smell. I know smells can trigger memories.'

'And did the smell in the room trigger a memory for you?' I ask.

'Yes. I know it sounds silly, but certain perfumes have always taken me back to one woman from my childhood – Akela.'

'Akela – as in Cubs and Scouts?' I enquire.

'Yes, Akela from my Cub pack. She was actually a friend of my mother's. She worked at one of the big department stores. She was a very good-looking woman – blonde, big breasts, you know the sort of thing. Akela worked on the perfume counter and there was always this strong smell of expensive perfume around her and in the Scout hall. Friday nights were exciting!' he says.

I'm curious as to why Marc seems to be taking us off at a tangent. In the opening minutes of the session he had clearly led me to believe there is some important material he wants to discuss, and yet each time he has approached it he has moved off in another direction.

'I enjoyed the Cubs,' he continues. 'I liked being with a different group of boys to those I mixed with at school and I always got this feeling around Akela.'

I decide to follow his lead. 'This feeling?' I ask. 'Do you mean a sexual feeling?'

'The smell of her, kind of knocked me out,' he replies 'a mix of perfume and cigarettes and … to watch her smoke held a certain fascination even in my prepubescent days so … yes, a sexual kind of feeling.'

'Did you masturbate about her?' I ask.

'Yes … sometimes … but I don't think I knew what I was doing at that age. It wasn't explicit sexual thoughts that I had running through my head. It was more like … more like it was with my primary school teacher.'

'Do you mean that you used to imagine that Akela was punishing you like you fantasized about Miss Pringle?' I ask, bringing up something he had told me in his fourth session.

'I don't know … I can't remember really.' Marc pauses. 'I have a dim memory of thinking about her holding my penis out in front of me, inspecting it and then me having to masturbate in front of the pack … it's fuzzy. Perhaps I used to think about her actually stroking my cock … I can't remember. I know she had a daughter, Sally. She was a year younger than me. When they came around to our house I used to chase Sally. She was a bit of a tomboy and didn't want to play girls' games with Simone. I can still remember her giggle – a screaming little giggle as she ran away from me. I even chased her into the bathroom once and bent her over the bath and spanked her with a table tennis bat I had been carrying around in my hand … wow … I haven't thought of that for years – pretty BDSM for a nine or ten year-old.'

'And it brings you back to spanking once more.' I wonder if I should follow him deeper into this childhood connection.

Silence …

I decide to test the water. 'So there are even more associations than you thought to spanking. You were also telling me about the smell you woke up to when you were sleeping with Louise. Last Saturday morning, Louise's perfume reminded you of Akela?'

'Yes, I was lying there in the middle of the night taking in the smell, trying to deconstruct it – vanilla, a hint of sugary apples, sandalwood and musk. It seemed like the smell was already hardwired in me. It was the smell of the perfume I gave Louise the first time we met and it was making me think of sex.'

'So, you seem to be saying that there was something about Akela that was "morphing" with Louise through the smell. Is there a physical resemblance between them as well?'

'Ha, no,' he chuckles. 'I'm not into blondes at all, especially not busty ones. Louise is a petite woman, about 5 foot 1, C cup breasts and beautiful long brunette hair – the opposite of Akela.'

'And the spanking connection? Akela's daughter, and yours and Louise's BDSM fantasies?' I enquire.

Marc sits still for a moment. He appears to be weighing something up. He scrunches his forehead a little as if to say: 'Do you want to hear this?'

Silence …

'Okay, when I woke early on Saturday, Louise was just laying there asleep next to me, her back showing to me. She had thrown the sheets off her shoulders so that most of her back was exposed. I gently stroked my hand across her skin. Then, as I put my hand lower down to rub her cheeks … instead of the smoothness … all I could feel were the raised welts … they were still raised hours after … where … where I had used a cane and a crop on her backside.'

Marc avoids my gaze as he talks.

'It's the first time I've ever beaten someone. It's what Louise has often asked me to do to her – in our telephone fantasies and in our online writing. She's so often asked me to beat or crop her; she's read me passages from *The Story of O* and De Sade that she likes. She says it gives her the deepest pleasure to be caned and cropped until welts rise on her cheeks; she says it gives her the strongest orgasms, somehow it releases her.'

'You seem pretty uncertain, Marc.'

'I just wanted to use my hand, to redden her cheeks. I felt … really confused … confused about really doing it … I felt … ashamed.'

Silence …

'Do you think you felt confused and ashamed because this is the sort of thing that happened to you and your sisters?' I ask him.

Silence …

'I liked it … I've looked at this sort of thing on the net and in magazines; I liked doing it to her, I enjoyed the power over her, but it also frightened me. What if I couldn't stop?'

We were heading into a complex and difficult area. Since the psychological ramifications for an individual who has been traumatized, especially during childhood, do not conform to a constant pattern of outcomes, but are highly individual, it leaves a therapist with a difficult path to tread. In many cases, therapeutic working through of the trauma is suitable. However, here are two people damaged by their childhoods who have come together, at least in the beginning, through sexual acting out. The dynamic is complex. Further to this, Marc has recently been traumatized by his contact with pornography and Louise has at least some unstable, if not borderline personality disorder, traits.

I guide him slightly with an interpretive question. 'It seems to me that you are saying that while you derived some pleasure from inflicting the marks and the pain on Louise, you also did not believe that this was really a consensual request on her part. You did not like the outcome. You enjoyed the act, but not the results of the beating you gave her?'

Marc thinks for a moment. 'Yes, that's right, but to cane, crop, beat someone – not like my mother did in anger, but for sexual stimulation – is a skilled job. I've never hit anyone like that before but Louise knew how she wanted it done, gave me a masterclass. So then it was like a skills workout but psychologically; once we were into it I felt quite spaced-out, as if I wasn't really doing it to her ... and I felt ... ashamed ... ashamed when I felt the marks on her the next morning.'

'And did you and Louise talk about it at all?'

'The worst thing is she thanked me for doing it to her. She said she felt really free and that she enjoyed the pain. She took a shower almost straight away after; she said that water made it sting more and that she was going to masturbate in the shower but only if I'd come and watch her.'

Silence ...

'It seems that beatings, spankings, punishment have been quite central to a lot of our work recently. Do you think you might be trying to say something about how you feel about it not only as an adult in this relationship with Louise but also how it felt as a child?'

'Ha, it seems to be yet another thing I don't know how I feel about. It does excite me to look at as fantasy, but doing that to Louise ... I don't know.' There is silence for a moment. 'Do you know Bettie Page?' Marc asks.

'The "notorious" Bettie Page – BDSM pin-up?' I reply.

'Yes, well her stuff was the first I ever saw in this area – another beautiful brunette,' Marc says.

Having written a paper that included some research into Page, I say to Marc, 'I saw an interview with her in the 1990s on US television. She always insisted that her infamous bondage photographs and films were not sexual.'

'Well, I'd love to be involved with it at that level,' Marc says, 'the look of it and the sensual control and pacing of it. Judy's quite happy to indulge in some fetishistic dressing up once in a while. But Louise was just asking me … to … to … abuse her …'

I think about the implicit sexual reference he made when he had spoken about his mother beating him. I risk bringing the two together: 'Does it all bring your own feelings up about being beaten and the question marks about a sexual reference with the way your mother used your underwear?'

'I guess it pulls in all that stuff I was telling you about Simone.'

Silence …

With his hand pushing through his hair he continues, 'Then it was the girl in the puffa jacket again … suddenly the bedroom was spinning, it felt like I couldn't swallow, I was in a cold sweat … it was just swirling around. I couldn't make any sense of it. It was like a photo album … just … pages flicking past my eyes … it was like an album of things I was ashamed of. My mother shouting at me, Simone was hissing at me to get out, with her knickers around her ankles, Louise was saying "Hurt me, harder, I want you to hurt my arse" … and then this smell of sex – the perfume, and I can smell this woman I'm in love with and yet suddenly I hated … God … "hated" … do I mean that? I leapt out of the bed and rushed to the bathroom.'

There are a thousand questions to ask Marc. *Why didn't you tell me what you were getting up to with Louise? Can I suggest Louise is not a good person to be with? How about Judy? Why am I giving* myself *such a hard time? What's in the transference here? Come on, what's my job? Am I here to fix this? Can Marc manage self-repair? Am I just here to walk alongside him? Do I trust him to fix himself? Is he really set to destruct? Am I taking Louise and Judy on as well through this process?*

At confusing times like this in the therapy space I find transparency a very useful tool. It allows a clear reflective possibility to say what I have heard and/or felt and gain clarification from the person in the process. *Tell it as you understand it.*

'It seems like you have started to piece some things together in your mind Marc, but it all seems to be at a traumatic level. I'm quite concerned for what you are going through. The connections you are making to your past are having quite an impact on your life in the present. To be honest with you, it feels like you are putting yourself in a very exposed and dangerous position with Louise and it seems to be causing you both more trauma.'

What will he make of that? Perhaps it's not easy for him to hear all those words and ideas right now?

Silence …

Marc looks at me, clearly holding a dialogue in his mind.

Silence …

'"Exposed and dangerous"? Do you really think so?' He says. *Interesting, what part he heard.* 'It certainly seems as if that is alive in the room, Marc; I'm aware right now that "exposed and dangerous" expresses a lot.' *That was just padding to avoid answering a question with a question. Will it do?*

'I'm so trapped. Can you get me out of here? It's getting worse isn't it.'

Silence …

'There's more I need to tell you about the weekend,' Marc looks pitiful as he speaks.

Yes, what you've been trying to say since the start of the session. I glance at the clock. *Time's still on our side; perhaps some containment will come from draining the tank. Let him go with it, at least for a while.*

I say to Marc, 'Well, time's on your side if there is more that needs telling.'

'We had a lovely day together. We walked along Brancaster Sands. You have to watch the tides there when you are on the beach but we spent ages with our shoes and socks off just paddling along the shoreline. But in the evening things got heavy.'

'Heavy?' I echo.

'Out of hand really. We settled into the living room. I'd just cooked some fresh fish we had bought. Louise said something like "You'll make someone a very good wife!" She poked me with her finger and then kissed me. That phrase just hit me – "a very good wife". We were in mine and Judy's living room. What in the fuck would she think if she saw this. I had sex with another woman in a bed we share. I walked like a teenager in the sea with a woman I keep saying I'm in love with. I said something like, "It's odd being here with you; it confuses me Lou. Where's this all going?" That was the beginning of it …' Marc scans my face; I intuit that this is not going to be an easy ride. '… and then she says to me, "Oh, here we go. Why can't we just be here, leave it at that?" Of course I made it much worse. It was like I was possessed by Judy. I said, "This is mine and Judy's house – somewhere we spend our Christmases together. I don't know that I should have brought you here." I knew it was a major mistake to say that out loud – I guess I was feeling guilty about what I was doing. She came back at me really sharp saying words to the effect of, "Hey buster, you sure know how to make an evening go with a swing! I didn't ask you to bring me here. In fact I've never asked you for anything apart from don't fuck with my feelings." Something like that.'

Marc tells me how they sat in silence for a while. How he knew he had done the wrong thing and that they were both upset.

'I was feeling really confused. I guess I was looking at Louise as a friend I could speak to, not as an insecure partner in something that suddenly felt like a crime to me.'

Marc continues to tell me how he wanted Louise to disappear at that moment. 'It was like someone had just switched my brain back on. Do you know that feeling when you come out of an anaesthetic? There's just a missing bit of time. It was like that. It was like I must have been going around looking and sounding like me but it was another version of me. Now I was seeing what I had been up to while I had been sedated.'

I decide not to interject. There are a number of concerns but there is such a strong feeling the next bit is the bit he wants to tell me that I stay silent. I take a slow deep breath, calming my system.

'Then she is saying, "I thought you brought me here because you trusted me, because you wanted to be with me. But no – I'm just being told I'm sharing you, I'm number two." The next thing I know is she has stood up and then she lunged at me. Instinctively I moved back as much as I could but she still caught me across my cheek and with the fingernail of her right hand she drew blood. I was so not expecting her to do that to me. I stood up for a moment. I wanted to run away. No, that's not quite true; for a split second – and you must believe me, it was just a split second – I wanted to … I wanted to smash her. Then she looks at me, horrified. I don't know if it was because of the blood on my face or if she could pick up my momentary desire to strike back at her.'

'You say you wanted to smash her.'

Silence …

'Yes … I felt like … what the fuck is this about?!'

'But didn't you know what it was about?'

'I guess I knew I had broken some kind of spell with my crass comments.'

'And that spell was suddenly broken for both of you?'

'I was never going to hit her. I never even hit my mother – and I could have done when I was a teenager. I could have knocked her out cold.'

'So you were never going to hit her but you stood up – half to run away, half to strike back?' I reflect and question him in one phrase.

'I just moved towards her and then she seemed really frightened of me. And she just steps back away from me. She says and then shouts, "Don't you fucking touch me, DON'T YOU TOUCH ME!" Her leg makes contact with the sofa and she is taken off balance and falls backwards onto it. She raises her arms across her face. Pulls her legs up to her chest into a ball. I could see she was terrified. Much that the nick to my cheek was a shock and it was stinging, I couldn't believe the reaction Louise was having to me. I felt like I was in a nightmare movie. Louise is still going on, "Don't you fucking touch me you cunt!" She's screaming. "Amy knows I'm with you, they'll get you, I know your fucking name – they'll find me, they'll find me you fucking creep, you can't hurt me any more."'

Silence …

The tension is not easing as yet. I know there is more to come. I am breathing slowly and deeply. I know Marc needs me to be detached from this story to hear it as an outsider.

He carries on his recall of the events: 'I'm just thinking how in the fuck have I got myself into this? The woman's a nutter. But then I just keep making it worse.'

I'm suddenly quite concerned, at a different level. Murderous rage is present. *Please tell me you've not done something really stupid, Marc. I've heard some awful things in this room over the years. Don't tell me you've snapped and that Louise is in the boot of your car parked outside and 'Would* [I] *be kind enough to phone the police and tell them it was an accident?'*

'I wanted to shut her up. So I grabbed her wrists in one hand so that I could then put a hand across her mouth. She screamed and I'm thinking, "You nutter. Back off; don't go forward. How in the fuck would this look if she went to the police. She knows this house. Look at what her arse looks like after last night. My DNA is under her fingernails and in her womb." And then she's struggled free, stood up and gone to the sideboard behind her, picked up the wine bottle and smashed it against the wall. Red wine is everywhere and so is the glass. I'm starting to panic. I'm a big lad but a mad woman with a bottle is not something I've faced before.'

Silence …

I break into the space as if to let Marc know I'm still there: 'It sounds like a very confused and fearful situation.'

'I started gabbling, "Lou, you've got this wrong; I'm not going to touch you, Lou, look at me. Look at me Skippy, what's going on sweetie? I'm not going to touch you, but you are scaring me now with that bottle in your hand." And suddenly she has stopped. It's like it was the first time we met. A blazing argument and then she is weeping and sobbing and I'm just melting inside for her. But she still had the bottle so I just said, "Put the bottle down sweetie, I'm not coming anywhere near you. You stay where you are and I'll stay here as well." She's saying, "Oh, God … oh … my God …" and I'm just focused on the bottle – "Can you put the bottle down Loulou."

'She drops it in front of her. Her face is pitiful – like the face of Munch's "Scream". "Can I come and pick up the glass Louise? I'm coming over to get the glass out of the way my love." I just worked as quickly as I could, picking up all the little bits of glass I could find and rushing them into the kitchen. I'm feeling like this is all my fault. I'm thinking how much I've hurt her. And I'm seeing her arse in my mind again. All I can think of is how she can't really make her mind up about things. God I thought I was fucked up but she takes it to another level.

'When I got back to her all I wanted to do was give her a hug. So I told her that's what I was about to do. She makes this wretched face and doesn't move as I squeeze her tight. I felt like I was trying to rescue her from drowning. She just let out a guttural cry as if something trapped in her for years was exiting her. The pain and terror of something unseen by me sort of rushed from her lungs.'

Silence …

Ten minutes from the end of the session, time to surface.

⋅⋗⋅ ⋅⋗⋅ ⋅⋗⋅

Marc and I debrief from the session. He has survived a week on his own and so, taking a calculated risk, it seems in the room that he will be able to survive and contain himself until Monday when we meet again. He has recounted his story of last weekend and there is a feeling that he has been honest both about what happened and how he felt. At the end of the session I am aware of how I feel like I am holding onto Louise as well as Marc. Having worked (in the past) in secure accommodation with very emotionally vulnerable women, I feel I know something about what Marc might have been confronted with.

We talk a little about how Louise had responded to what she saw as a threat to them as a couple. I suggest to Marc that she saw it as an emergency that required immediate defensive action rather than thought or conversation. The rise to the surface was not the time to talk in detail about post-traumatic stress disorder.

Marc tells me that despite the awfulness of the situation in the living room last Saturday, Louise had settled down quite quickly after he had begun to hug her and although neither of them slept very well that night they spent the time in the bedroom hugging each other and being close.

Marc tells me how they had continued to talk for the rest of the weekend about both of their issues, about the abuse they had suffered as children; Louise also told Marc much more about the two abusive marriages she had survived. They had agreed that they would find new ways to explore together their sexual needs – ways that did not parallel their abusive pasts. Finally, just before we end the session, rising from our seats and shaking hands as we do on parting, Marc tells me they had not had much contact with each other this week. Although I hear his words describing how they had both 'reassured each other that this was okay' my intuition suggests this is anything but true. As I watch the gate close behind Marc I can't help my mind chase an image of Louise, alone. *Poor Loulou.*

12 thank god tomorrow's friday

13 September 2007

WELCOME TO OUR ISLAND

Skippy: *from x.x.x111 joined the chat 30 mins ago*
Skippy: So, on here again all by myself!!! I've got to say I'm not feeling good about keep talking to myself!

Skippy: It feels pretty bad that you hardly pick up your phone these days – guess that should be a message to me …

Skippy: I'll give it a few more mins then I'm off.

Skippy: This is making me angry.

Skippy: Still here 16.25h.

The Don: *from x.x.x63 joined the chat*
The Don: You still here?

Skippy: Why?

The Don: Don't be like that.

Skippy: Be like what?

The Don: Hang on, reading you …

The Don: OK, beautiful …

The Don: I'm up to speed – I can see you have a cob on.

The Don: LOL

Skippy: Fuck you! NOT LOL

The Don: Sorry, I've been very busy

The Don: and my mobile's on the blink.

Skippy: Fuck you! Don't insult me – I thought you were an intelligent man! You can come up with a better excuse than that! This is just such a fucking mess now, and …

Skippy: you are pissed off with me

Skippy: and me with you!

The Don: You feel I'm pissed off with you?

Skippy: You must be, I'm wasting your time here – isn't that what u think?

Skippy: I don't know how much I can take of being with you Marc. You are so much what I want but the thought that you still belong to someone else – the thought that you don't need a silly bitch like me just plays on my mind sometimes.

The Don: Uhh??

Skippy: I didn't mean to hit you, and I certainly didn't mean to cut you. Thought you understood that – forgave me, I thought you said.

The Don: I have, it was an 'accident'

The Don: but we are both pretty fucked up people. I woke up this morning. I had a sort of panic attack! So much for bloody therapy!

Skippy: What you fucking about with therapy for, never did me any good. You'll just end up with a label on you and that will be that.

The Don: You're my real therapist – my physical therapist mwwhhh!

Skippy: Hey! STAY WITH THIS!

Skippy: I get the feeling I'm just your plaything when you do that. I'm not asking you to leave JJ or anything but I do want you to really be with me you know. It's been almost three weeks since we went to your place. Hardly a peep out of you snice.

Skippy: God, I tripe well! – since

The Don: Mwwhhh. A big hug. I know you panicked that night. You thought I was dumping you or something.

Skippy: Is that your therapist talking now!

The Don: Oh come on! Lighten up a bit! It's not my therapist it's me.

The Don: Look, we've been through this before

The Don: that morning I had been stroking your back, as you were asleep. You felt so beautiful but then as I slid my hand down onto your bum

The Don: I could still feel the welts were raised on your arse. Look, this is new to me. I realize it made me think about the way my mother abused me (and my sisters). I've just started to talk about that in some depth in therapy …

The Don: but that morning I was stuck inside all my past feelings and also that fucking video of the Eastern European girl I told you about. It was like after you blew up – it felt like I had abused you.

Skippy: It's what I wanted you to do to me. I told you that then and I'm telling you that now as well. I need it to be painful in order for me to get the orgasm I want.

Skippy: That's why I wanted you to bugger me in front of the mirror the first time we met. I wanted you to stick it straight in, no warm-up stretch, just you forcing it into me while I looked at it happening to me.

The Don: Louise, that's just your ABUSE again. That's how those bastards did it to you when you were a kid. I don't want to be part of that – that's why the puffa girl sticks in my mind. I can't stand that that happened to you.

Skippy: No, it's what I wanted you to do to me then I wanted/want you to hug me in the painful feelings, in the tears after it all, I want to be held by you, hug me better, kiss me, stroke me how you did that morning. IT IS MY CHOICE and I don't want you to take that away from me. The hugs make the pain go away.

Skippy: I didn't however want you to beat me up. I don't like being punched and kicked. I didn't ask you to bring around three or four of your mates and force me to suck you all off, deep throat you or get raped in my pussy and arse one after another, THAT'S ABUSE.

The Don: But my mother beat me like I caned and cropped you last time we met. I was going back over stuff with my therapist last week and saying more about what I remember. How there are connections for me and you with my childhood stuff – seeing Simone, all that.

Skippy: I don't know if I like you talking about me to a fucking therapist

Skippy: Anyway, that's YOUR abuse Marc, not mine.

The Don: I'm getting angry. So it's ok for me to live through my abuse again as long as it GETS YOU TO CUM. Is that what you are saying – you getting off is what really matters …?

Skippy: It's O.K. for you to control how I get my orgasms is it? You control what kinda sex I should have is it!

Skippy: God, you can be such a fucking prick sometimes. I thought you were kidding me about not knowing how to give out a good beating. All your talk on the phone line, thought you were a player and you just turned out a limp prick.

The Don: I was fucking abused as well you know!

The Don: *logged off*

Fucking whore. Marc smashes his fist on his desk. He picks up his briefcase and walks to his PA's office.

'I'm off for the day now Sarah – I'll be in at ten tomorrow.'

'Okay Marc. Is everything okay?'

'Yes, I'm fine just a bit of a migraine coming on I think.'

'Do you want someone to drive you home?'

'Oh no, nothing like that.'

'You sure you're up to driving Marc? I'll drive you myself.'

'No it's fine Sarah, thanks. See you in the morning.'

'Okay, see you tomorrow then – hope it's not a bad one.'

Marc drives dangerously on his way home from the office. He undertakes several cars on the dual carriageway and motorway that leads out of Cambridge towards the quiet village he lives in. His mind is consumed by thoughts of Louise. He feels a rage towards her that is unlike anything he has been aware of before. For a moment, when the driver of a car he undertakes shows him his middle finger, Marc considers ramming the car off the road. *You don't know how fucking lucky you are that I don't take you and me out right now …* 'Nothing to lose here, CUNT!' he shouts at the top of his voice, 'Fucking cunt – I could destroy you, you fucking wanker.'

▄▖ ▖▄▖ ▖▄▖

Marc has spoken in the therapy space of how he is worried about the effect Louise is having on him. It has been almost three weeks since they last met and for much of that time he has been trying to withdraw from the relationship with her. But he finds that the smallest contact with her seems to pull him back into the web of their joint creation. In a session he says, 'It will probably have to be her who breaks up our relationship.'

5.12pm Adrenaline is still flooding Marc's system as he opens the browser of his laptop. He lies down on the bed and rests the laptop on his chest. For a moment he is about to log back on to the Island and let Louise know what he really thinks of her but his frustration at not being able to express himself, other than through anger, draws him to search for pornography.

He types the address of the biggest site he knows. Once the browser opens to the home page he enters 'pain + rape + spank + beat + abuse + brunette' into the search box. The site returns thirty-two pages relevant to the search terms. Marc is looking for a movie that will play out his internal vision. Among the thumbnail picture links of <u>Ballgagged brunette getting her ass destroyed</u>, <u>Big titted darkhaired beauty gets her pussy electrocuted</u> and <u>Slavegirl brutally caned til she screams</u>, Marc finds an image of a woman that is a good enough likeness for Louise. The caption to the link reads <u>Butcher's hook warms up bitch's hole for an anal fisting</u>. Marc clicks the image and the browser begins to load the clip. First the caption appears at the top of the frame.

> This sexy brunette knows that the more it hurts the better she cums. First she is stripped naked and bound to the bench before her master places a hook in her asshole. Then he whips her before she is taught how to open up her asshole for a lesbian fisting.

Marc has administered himself the only analgesic he knows and his orgasm comes quickly. Before he ejaculated he had been full of hatred. Certain, for the period it had taken him to drive home, that Louise was the seat of all his problems. But now, as the blissed-out relief of his orgasm fades, he simply feels alone. He feels sorrow for himself. Like a little boy abandoned, he feels the fear of being alone in a world that is too big to be understood.

Marc is crying. At first he is simply aware that moisture is leaking from the corner of his eyes but as he becomes more aware, his tears well more quickly. The feeling in his gut tells him that the 'welling' is to be feared and yet he does not resist it. He lets the fear in his belly rise to his head and overtake his entire body.

In the bedroom there is an unfamiliar noise that Marc gradually notices; moment by moment into his consciousness creeps the fact that the noise is emanating from him. He exclaims out loud: 'I remember. I do remember – oh God, I remember.'

5.58pm Marc enters his study. He takes down the book with his sex SIM attached and replaces his standard mobile SIM card with it. The phone switches back on and after a few seconds three text messages come through in quick succession.

> **Marc fone me plse Lxxx**
>
> **Marc I love U plse fone me Lxxx**
>
> **Marc I need you now plse dont leave.
> There are thngs 2 say darling, sorry...
> Fone me xxxLxxx mwh**

He dials Louise's number.

'Marc! Mwwhhhh, I'm sorry. I'm so sorry. I'm such an insecure bitch ...' she pauses '... it's just I keep realizing I only rent you from JJ. I don't want to mess up what we've got. I want to be with you. I don't want to break you and JJ up, I just want to be with you once in a while. Mwwhhh, I love you but I *can* share you.'

There is silence before Marc speaks. His delivery is thoughtful, pausing, slow. 'I'm sorry as well. But I really do need to have a little bit of time … at the moment.'

'NO!' Louise retorts – desperately. 'You're breaking up with me aren't you?' She begins to cry.

Marc speaks more quickly. 'No Loulou. Just give me some time for a day or two. I promise I'm not breaking up with you. I've just driven home like a wanker, I've just looked at stuff on the Internet that I want to get away from and I've just remembered something I don't want to talk about with anyone right now – not with you, not with JJ, not with anyone.'

'I can tell you are dumping me,' Louise sobs.

'No, I love you Loulou, I really do, I'm not leaving you but please let me go right now – tonight. Give me to Saturday and I'll be back online.'

'But, I know you are just trying to be kind …' With the tone of a toddler in a tantrum she continues, 'I can tell by the way you left the Island by how long it's taken for you to return my texts, my messages. You've had your fun with me.'

'Lou we are both upset and angry at the moment …'

Louise interrupts Marc. 'You're fucking dumping me.' Her voice is now very angry.

'Shut the fuck up!' Marc interrupts her. 'LISTEN,' he shouts. 'If you don't listen I'll put the phone down now.'

'CUNT!' Louise shouts back and hangs up.

6.57pm Marc has returned to the Internet and browsed to extreme porn images. He walks around the house with his laptop, not particularly registering the images he is sorting through. He is not aroused by any of the clips or pictures he is looking at. Finally sitting down, he thinks of Louise as he registers how much the light has faded in the sky. The timer switch system has turned on some of the lights in the downstairs of the house giving the appearance to the outside that life is happily proceeding at number 2 Mill Lane.

Marc takes a bottle of Peroni from the chill cabinet in the kitchen and begins to drink it. His mind is full of the particular memory that the events of the afternoon have triggered. Judy has just texted him to say that she will be 'home in 15 mins'. Marc opens the fridge door and pulls out some wet fish, new potatoes, broccoli. He washes the vegetables, places the potatoes and broccoli in separate saucepans. He turns the hob rings on. Like an automaton he pours some oil into a cold frying pan. *Thank God tomorrow's Friday*, he thinks. *Therapy.*

13 *star trek* was on the TV

'So at least for a moment, your thoughts had been so negative that you looked at Louise as if she actually was a prostitute. Were you thinking of her as '*your* whore', as a possession, as a woman conquered and dominated?'

'Good question … ummh … no, I think … I think I really meant it in the way of derogatory comment and thought towards a woman who was being a bitch to me. I think I was setting myself up – above her; that she was, at least for a moment,' he motions air quotes, 'a "worthless bitch" I wanted to destroy before she made any attempt on me.'

We have trodden a course back to Marc's mother many times and despite the fact that I could see some profitable connections that might be made to her here, it is the sense of relief of Marc admitting the way he had thought towards Louise as a woman that is of most interest. This is a solid glimpse of his internal view of women – not the one he wants me to see, not the façade he erects. I am aware there is even a chance that I might be able to reflect to him how he craves me to collude with him and join in his unreconstructed, old-school masculinity – at least at some level.

Despite the intellectual possibilities for us to engage with work on gender and power right now, intuition leads the way once more and I stay silent for a long while, paused like a cat waiting for a passing butterfly. When it seems clear that Marc is not going to add further comment I prompt him.

'And so, when you got home, the video clip you found of the restrained brunette who gets hoisted and penetrated and all the rest became what you wanted to do to Louise. It became the punishment you realized you did want to give to her?' (I am still tempted by the opportunity to bring a connection to his mother.) 'But was it aimed at Louise alone?' I ask.

'Shit! My head's going to explode if I don't say this next bit, but yes, yes I guess what you are saying is spot on. After all that though …'

There is a very long pause.

Perhaps I should have kept my powder dry there. He's going to go on the run again.

All the energy of engagement with Marc and Louise's story that was building in the room is somehow removed and replaced with a tangible feeling of anxiety and tension.

No, not on the run – something powerful again. That feeling's in the gut – roller-coaster ride ahead?

'After all that, after I'd … masturbated, in the short window where it feels like everything's just been let go of after you cum, I could remember something I've often been so very uncertain of …'

There is another long silence.

'A few sessions ago I was telling you about Akela and you asked me about my sexual feelings towards her. I knew it then … for certain I knew it then … but it was so far back and then I remember thinking *there's no way I'm ever going to bring it forward again.* But this fuck-ing mess with Loulou … I don't know … I just don't see why it's come up now … I think I hoped that it wasn't this … that it really did have something to do with the op even when I know it didn't. I don't want it to be this … I don't know how to say it. It can't actually be said out loud … how can a son say such things …?'

Marc's sentences are disjointed. This is his internal record, not for external consumption. I am cast as outsider. I stop trying to second-guess the content, the direction of his words. I stop trying to make sense of his thoughts; I fall back to a suspended listening technique – picking up the tone, texture, timbre of the monologue. I listen for what words want to be heard, connected with.

Where in my body should I feel these utterances? This is really gripping my guts quite deeply now, Marc. It quite literally feels like you are 'shit scared'.

I breathe.

'Marc, are you trying to tell me something about what your mother did to you?'

One minute struggles around the clock.

The volume is cut to silence but the work is still continuing for us both.

'I don't know if they were really Mondays, but that's how I remember them. *Star Trek* was on the TV.'

Silence.

'I was still quite young you know, seven, no I think I was eight by this time? But anyway still a little kid. Ronny and Simone were out of the house; they went to their piano lessons. My father was always keen to take them to their music lessons. He said he always regretted not being able to play an instrument so we all learned something – I hated it. Anyway, it was just my mother and me in the house.'

The pressure in my own body is enormous at this moment. Monitoring myself I'm aware that I actually feel slightly dizzy with the adrenaline that is pumping. I focus on my breath for a second; the air comes in more deeply. I calmly brush my thumb on the back of my hand – stroking myself. The movement is imperceptible to Marc but my system responds to the message it receives through this micro movement. His mention that his sisters were out of the house I take to be the first signifier of what is to come; like the beginning of the scary music underscore in a horror movie, I know almost certainly what I am about to hear.

I have prepared my system so that I can remain fully present for Marc as he tells me what I anticipate to be the most awful memory of his childhood. The previous eighteen sessions of preparation, containment and modelling are barely adequate for the thing I believe he is about to tell me, something still so taboo in society. Although I am convinced of the content, the specific details of what he is about to tell me will be unique to him.

'You asked me a while back about times when my mother might have been nice to me.' Marc's voice is small, thin, the pitch raised a little. His watery eyes glance towards me and I am further captured in the transference of his story. Marc is a small child in front of me.

'Those Monday evenings were times when there was this feeling of tenderness from my mother.'

As I'm thinking about this, I'm aware that the work we did on the *macro* world might have something to do with this memory coming up right now.

A delay at the point of disclosing something is becoming a trademark for Marc. He is in obvious pain and broadcasting his anxieties in the room when he switches focus. Although it is a relatively common thing that people do at such times, Marc seems to be developing it into an art form. But this time, I am also intrigued by his diversion since the *macro conversation* technique I used with him is at my own current developmental edge as a therapist.

•••• •••• ••••

The *macro conversation* is a simple non-technical 'tool' that can act as a 'therapy brake' in trauma work. Through a focus on a particular year or years in history (from the viewpoint of the actual social history as remembered by an individual), types of sweets/chocolate bars, changes in coinage, the arrival of the home PC, for example, all become the spoken of, extrinsic, 'characters' of the dialogue. These *macro* objects allow a safer route for patients into the historical period in which traumatic events took place without the need to remember the most heavily recorded, but most defended, details of that era – the abuse (or trauma itself).

•••• •••• ••••

I don't want my own interest to get in the way of facilitating Marc to tell me his remembered but unspeakable event. But what was it the *macro conversation* brought up? The memory of an object? A particular occasion?

'I'm sorry,' Marc seems to plead at me, 'can I just use the toilet?'

There are twenty minutes left in the session as Marc sits back down in the chair opposite me. In the time he has been out of the room I have weighed up the options that feel possible. I know myself not to be prepared to take the risk of labelling what might have happened to him, even though it feels as if this is what he is hoping I will do. *I'm certain of the subject matter; why won't I help him to label this? Am I scared of this subject? What's it close to? Come on, he's hardly the first to disclose it in the room.*

◆◆◆ ◆◆◆ ◆◆◆

Marc's expectations of himself and the recovery process are often too great. Although he has begun to make some progress with his use of pornography, his life is still in free fall. He seems unable to take responsibility for his actions; he appears unable to face up to his own part in the proceedings of his life. Without a doubt, he is a victim of many things. But he is also capable, and through his own hard work (plus his inheritances), he has become a privileged man. But here we both sit, challenged by where to go and what to say. For the first time in our work together I feel a little lost. It seems there is something to do, a direction to take, one that sits so pregnant, one he has set up and yet we can only walk there, together, if he takes the next step.

I sit in silence.

'Okay, I can do this. I'm going to start this *macro* style, saying it like we talked before. The empty set is being filled up with the props of this childhood room. This room will look like the place this bad stuff happened in – but it won't be the real room. I will always be in charge. This is my own creative space. Okay. I'm sat on the sofa next to mother. I can see the dark wood coffee table in front of me. There's a green cushion between us. The big new colour TV is on. It's one of the first times I've seen *Star Trek* in colour. The walls are white; the sun's going down and shining through the net curtains. The standard lamp's on. She moves her hand lower on my tummy, and her finger runs up and down the waistband of my underwear. Her fingernails are quite long and the varnish from the weekend is still bright. I can see her red fingernails disappearing in and out of the elastic. I'm sort of frozen to the green cushion. She feels warm, nice, but I've also got this sort of fear in me. My jaw's all tight. Then it happens.' Marc takes a pause.

Silence.

I remain motionless – imagining what it might have felt like to have been that small boy at that moment in time. I feel helpless again, since it feels as if without the next sentence from Marc any utterance from me would destroy what he is trying to describe and stay in control of. I breathe as deeply and audibly as I dare, as if to communicate I am here and I am alive – with him, looking at the *mise-en-scène* he has created.

He continues.

'Her finger moves deeper into my underwear and her finger brushes against my … penis. I can remember thinking this wasn't right. I had been circumcized when I was six because of repeated infections and I ended up with some complications after the procedure. It meant I had to have cream applied to the head of my penis, and my mother was involved with some dressings and things because I had persistent bleeding. I was embarrassed then. She made me feel like I'd lose my penis if I didn't do exactly what I was told. I had nightmares for a while about a bird that came in the night and pecked off my penis.' Marc mimes a visible shiver down his back. 'But this was different. First she brushed my penis then, when I didn't react to her, she took it to be some kind of sign that … that it …' Marc's voice cracks, 'that it was okay to touch me … She circled its head with her index finger. When I still did not move she began to pinch it between her thumb and index finger. She kneaded it between her fingers until the blood began to flow. It was like I was out of my body. I was having an erection while she squeezed my penis and I watched *Star Trek*. I don't think she looked at me once; she didn't say a word. It would have been like nothing was happening to look at our faces, but at waist level my mother was masturbating her eight year-old son.'

Silence.

I breathe audibly. Marc looks at me. I sigh and screw up my face. There are no words.

Silence.

'Do you need to say more? Do you need more silence? Do you need me to talk?'

Silence.

'I have more.' Marc speaks quickly now as if squeezing the words out before a door closes. 'A few weeks later it happened again – only the second time it was much worse. When I was erect she said something like, "This probably sounds odd but the doctor told me that we should do this. It's okay to do this because I am checking that your tail" – it's what I called my penis as a child – "works properly after your operation." She said something about how the doctor had told her to wait until I was seven or eight to do this. My mother also said I could have gone to the surgery and done this with him. God, the thought of that was terrifying. But *I* knew everything was okay with me. I masturbated every night before I went to sleep.

'Then I began to wonder if I had damaged myself. I thought that perhaps I should have waited until now to allow myself to become erect. I thought that perhaps my mother would know by looking at me that I had been masturbating. I worried about the "doctors and nurses" games I had played with my sister and friends. But most of all I was worried that if I didn't let my mother do this then I'd have to go to the doctor, who was a man, and let him do it.

'I knew there was something wrong – very wrong – with what she was saying but I wanted a man to do this to me even less than my mother. I was still confused by what sex was about. But since I knew it felt nice to run around my bedroom with my penis erect in front of Adele I thought what my mother was doing couldn't have been that wrong or something. I don't know. I was very confused by it all. My mother said she had told the doctor it would be kinder if she "did the test". Then she told me that lots of people don't know this is what has to happen after an operation like mine – when there had been complications – so I should not bother them about this. There was a particular tone about what she said. I knew I needed to say, "I won't" like a good boy or there would be something to come from her. Then all I can remember is that I was standing in front of her ... my trousers and pants at my ankles and my penis out in front of me. I knew this was wrong in the same way that I knew Simone and our friends shouldn't take our clothes off for each other, but somehow I didn't know this was sexual. I knew not to protest or question mother, though. She prodded and poked at it and pronounced that it looked good enough to eat. I was terrified at that and then … she … she … moved forward … and kissed my penis … she put her lips on it … she kissed it then … she … then she sucked it.' Very quickly he added, 'That's all I can remember.'

Silence.

•+• •+• •+•

Having been born in the mid-1960s I am a man who has been influenced greatly in his life by the feminist issues that raged during my formative years. I have lived all my days in a society with the idea (even if not the practice) of equality of the sexes.

Marc's disclosure of his mother as a sexual abuser brings a much more uncomfortable idea of 'equality' – females as abusers. Although women and mothers as sexual abusers appear, in the literature and my professional experience, to be rare, Marc's case is not unique.

According to a study undertaken for the NSPCC in 2000 of young adults surveyed about their childhood, 49 per cent of those in the study had experienced violent treatment from their mother (and 40 per cent from their father). I'm sure that this too flies in the face of popular myths about fathers and mothers. Indeed, in the face of it many of us might even find a desire to block out such evidence, to fall back on the vestiges of the deeply ingrained idea that men are the aggressors and women the gentle caregivers. Men get drunk and come home and beat their wives and children, and while this is, of course, sometimes true, it seems that this idea is then partnered by the idea that it is important that society must continue to see most (even all) women as timid, fearful and vulnerable (though clearly this is not true). Marc has told me that not only was his mother a psychological bully and a physical abuser but also she breaks what might be the final taboo – she is a sexually abusive mother.

•+• •+• •+•

The session has reached its end. Marc and I have sat in silence for a few minutes, allowing the intensity of the material to dissipate. He signals that it is okay to rise to the surface and communicate again when he pours himself a glass of water from the bottle on the side table. The final words of the session said, we reach our parting. Marc shakes my hand at the threshold to the door. We underline the importance of the 'ceremony' – the acceptable contact between two people who have travelled some distance together.

'Have a nice weekend.'

'I'll see you on Monday,' I respond. 'You know the contact system if you should need it.'

Marc pauses outside of my room for a moment. 'Yes, thank you, I shan't need it … but thank you.'

14 it's been a long road

18 October 2007

'I'm sorry, your card won't go through.'

'Can you try it again?'

'I've tried it twice – you really do need to speak to your bank about it.'

'Well, I don't have any cash … I'll have to leave it all then.'

'Sorry, Miss.'

Louise's weekly shopping is bagged up at the end of the conveyor belt. *Fuck. Fucking overdraft. Shit! Shit! Shit!*

Louise exits the mini-market and walks to the newsagent, which has a cash machine outside. She mentally crosses her fingers. Enters her PIN: 7, 4, 1, 6. The machine makes a clunking sound and then the inevitable message flashes across the screen. *Fuck you!*

Like a kick-boxer she lifts her leg and slams her foot onto the keypad and into the screen of the bank machine and then, squatting to the floor, she bursts into tears. With her heel still throbbing, Louise walks back to her house at the end of a rather grubby street. The paint on the front gate is peeling and a hinge is broken, so she has to lift the gate to open it. She has asked David many times if he can come and fix it for her, but he has not. She teases him that 'it's nice to have a gay son to go shopping with' but she would have liked 'a straight one as well' to sort out the DIY problems.

The house is silent as she enters. The nights are drawing in quickly now and it leaves the empty house seeming even colder. Every time Louise returns to her home she mourns the loss of Amy's buoyant teenage spirit; it seems everybody else has a house she would rather spend time in.

6.39pm Louise has a few minutes before she has to log on for work. She goes to her PC to check her account. *Shit! I'm never going to get straight.* She clasps the fingers of one hand to the bridge of her nose and pinching tight slides them down to its tip. She clicks on to the Island.

WELCOME TO OUR ISLAND

Skippy: *from x.x.x111 joined the chat*
Skippy: Well, I see no messages from you Marc. Seems like I have lost you this time. Fits with my shit life at the moment.

Skippy: Don't even know if you will ever even come and read what I'm writing now.

Skippy: You talked of the way you loved me

Skippy: but now you just ignore me.

Skippy: There will be some reason that you give me

Skippy: but truth is I don't really exist for you do I?

Skippy: I guess I was a voice at the end of the phone, a quick wank for you.

Skippy: I bet you laugh at me and how pathetic I am. I bet you look down at me from your great height and wet yourself that I'm so gullible. You had me, fucked me, used me. You promised me all kind of things.

Skippy: Then what did you really give me …

Skippy: Sweet Fanny Adams.

Skippy: You said how important and special I was to you because I could listen, that I could help you. But then you went to therapy and that was the end of me.

Skippy: Because I COULD understand you, you turned and ran.

Skippy: Well, all I can say to you is that you are no better than the rest of them. You used me for your own fun and then when I wanted things from you, you couldn't give them to me.

Skippy: You are such a sissy you know, any real man would have known how to use that cane on me.

Skippy: Well the bitch is up and running now. You'll find out. You should have put me in my place when you had the chance. You should have raped me like the rest. You should have hit me good and hard that night when I cut you.

Skippy: If you were here right now you'd be the one tied up, face down. I'd have prepared a tabletop for you. There would be a hole in it just where your cock would fit. You'd be strapped to the table with your pathetic little cock poking through the hole. I'd take hold of your balls and squeeze them until you really knew what pain was like.

Skippy: I'd twist them until you thought I was going to rip them off your body. Then I'd get some big old gay boy to come and rape you. I'd not do it myself in case you enjoyed it but some ugly old gay would make you want to puke in fear. You really did turn out to be the biggest piece of shit I ever came across.

Skippy: I can't believe what I thought of you. How you had my heart more than any man ever did. How I wanted to be loved right back like I loved you. You say that JJ does not understand you. That she is distant and uncaring – well, take a look around Donkey man, your cocks too small to please any woman and your heart is even smaller.

Skippy: You do not see what you have and no matter how worthless a person you might have turned out to be, youz still a beautiful looker. When we've been together, I've seen the girls and boys look at you

– the chamber maid, the waitress, the receptionist, the barman they all looked at me as if to say How the fuck did YOU get him!

Skippy: Everyone's got their hands down their knickers thinking about you.

Skippy: I bet you thought there was nothing around when we went up to Norfolk to let me see the inside of your life. I bet you don't know I know you live at 2 Mill Lane. Bet you thought I'd never see those photos of JJ.

Skippy: I'm getting to be one for the girls, you know, and she is beautiful. I'd get my tongue in her twat and give her a better time than you ever could, she'd be a lot happier with what I could do to her than you ever can.

Skippy: SO, you are beautiful, JJ is beautiful, your house in Mill Lane is beautiful, your car is beautiful, and I take it those are your two grown-up children in that photo with you, if so they are beautiful too. In fact, everything in your life is beautiful ON THE OUTSIDE. But inside you're full of rotting stinking mess. You are full of the shit and the rubbish of humanity.

Skippy: I expect you stopped reading this ages ago – if you even started reading it. I bet you panicked when you realized I've got all your details, all your life logged. And you, you never even found out my surname Marc Moreau of number 2 Mill Lane! Yes, I have your home telephone number. What's worse for you is that I have JJs mobile number and yes, it is the right one because she has such a sweet little message on her voicemail.

Skippy: You should be fucking her over the phone. Her voice is sweet and horny, I bet all the men in her office cream themselves to her voice on the phone. Marc, she probably works for a sexline herself part-time. I bet you'd not even recognize her if you heard her on the phone line.

Skippy: But what do you know of me Marc? That my daughter's name is Amy and my son is David? Yes, that's true. The ashtray on wheels reg number so you can track me down? Of course not, you could hardly look at 'her'. Where do I live? You just don't know. You were never that interested in me Marc.

Skippy: It took a longtime for me to see all this. You know, until I started writing this down even I didn't know how much I knew about you. Oh yes, there's more. You don't know about me because I'm not worth all the extra effort. You just wanted to get off, cum over the phone, cum over the computer, cum over what you thought was me. You just wanted to fuck me, abuse me like all the rest.

Skippy: Skippy, Loulou, Louise, Lou, which one am I Marc?

Skippy: I'm in trouble now; my life is a mess again. I've got no money, no food, bills to pay. I can't work any more hours on the lines. I've got a friend who tells me there is still some good money to make in a parlour she has been working in for a while. So, perhaps I'll get some respect for myself and sell what I seem to have been giving you for nothing.

Skippy: You know, I'm knocking on a bit but the creeps out there will cream themselves quick enough when I wrap my fist around their cock, close my lips over them or open my holes for them.

Skippy: Oh, and if you are still reading this…

Skippy: This is a poem I had written for you a while back. I guess it shows what a silly bitch I really am – clearly just an idiot for rent.

Skippy: It's a long road that we have journeyed on

Skippy: And so often I have wanted to turn and run

Skippy: But now I know where this route is leading

Skippy: The island I've only seen in my dreams.

Skippy: ****

Skippy: No longer will the sun fade from my sight,

Skippy: No longer will I see an empty space by my side

Skippy: Because I have a soul next to me

Skippy: Because I have a soul to walk in my footstep

Skippy: *****

Skippy: You were by me when I cried for what I lost

Skippy: And so now, I keep your love locked inside

Skippy: It's been a long road that we have journeyed on

Skippy: But no longer do I feel the need to turn and run.

Skippy: Well, beautiful Marc, That's it from me. I need to leave now because it's bad for my self esteem to stay. I just missed the cue that you were already gone. Silly bitch, stupid and gullible that I am. Go on have a laugh with your mates.

Skippy: I won't be back, good night and good by – so long and thanks for the journey, I can see my stop right now.

Skippy: *left the chat 18.59*

Stop snivelling you stupid cow. You were actually the one who chose this end. Yes, you can check back later and see if the stupid cunt leaves a message. One fucking step wrong now and you can talk to JJ. Ohhh, wicked plan Lou.

·•· ·•· ·•·

Louise logs on to the chatline system, enters her PIN and waits for the phone to ring.

7.03pm 'Yes, baby, you can stick it anywhere you like – I won't feel a thing, ohh yes … Yes, stick it in baby… oh yes I like it like that … oh it's so big … oh yes … give me it … oh … oh … that's so good …'
    The telephone is put down.
    Fucking prick time waster …
    Louise's phone chirps that a text has arrived. She picks the phone up and reads the message. It's Marc, saying that he is on the Island.

7.10pm 'Yes, I do anal … is that what you want … oh yes, stick it in there … you can do it in both holes yes … oh it's so big … oh yes … that's hot … Yes, stick it in baby… oh yes … give me it … oh … oh … that's so good …'
    The telephone is put down.
    At least you said thanks.

7.18pm 'Yes, you can sniff them … is that what you want … oh yes, put your nose right in them … They're navy blue of course … Oh, sir, you are so big … I've never seen such a big one … oh, it's so big … oh yes … that's hot … Yes, stick it in, sir… please don't hurt me … oh … oh … that's so good… I will sir, would you like my PIN number …'
    Fucking cheeky cunt!

7.36pm 'Hi Pete, back to the best bitch in the business then … I think it's too small to get it in there … is that what you want Pete … well, perhaps you could just start with three or four fingers my love … Well you know I've taken a fist in my pussy, you slipped it in last time we spoke … yes …'

Louise's phone chirps again. She picks it up and reads the message as she talks.

Xxx lou xxx I'm leaving my message up for 24 hrs & then unless u tell me otherwise I'll take the island down. Pls read my message xxx Mxxx

'… but I don't think you could get one in my arse … please don't … no it hurts, please no, I can't take it there. Oh, you sweet man, that's better … I knew you wouldn't hurt me … oh … oh … that's so good …' Louise laughs out loud. 'Yes, I'm still on the same times … Pleasure … any time Pete.'

8.40pm 'Get something else to do idiot.'

8.41pm 'Well it's not exactly what people ask for everyday … Okay they are rolled up, how's that … but if I put them in there you might not be able to hear what I say … oh … ohhh … ahh … ahhh … ohh … ohhh …'

9.03pm 'Hello sweetie, why are you whispering? … She's asleep next to you … mwwhh … oh that's so nice … I love it when you do that … but won't she wake up … mwwhhh … Oh she's awake … oh, so now she's playing with herself in front of you … mwwhh … You'd like her to lick me … that's so hot … You want her to lick my arse hole … that's good.'

9.54pm 'Yes – fuck you too arsehole.'

9.56pm 'Oh piss off with your teenage games you idiot.'

9.58pm 'You thick or something; it's costing *you* money to be an idiot, not me.'

10.09pm 'Yes, of course I do anal … is that what you want … oh yes, you can stick it in me as deep as you like … oh you naughty boy sticking it in one hole and then the other … you feel rather big back there … yes, you're so big … oh yes … that's hot … Yes, stick it in baby…'

•+· •+· •+·

7.05pm Marc logs in to the Island.

WELCOME TO OUR ISLAND

The Don: *from x.x.x63 joined the chat 6 mins ago*
The Don: Bugger missed you by 6 mins.

The Don: Wow, just read you. Read it all Loulou. Is this the point our worlds changed? Missed the whole event by 6 minutes.

The Don: The Don is in shock but of course, you are right.

The Don: I'm going to text you so that you know I really am writing this now.

The Don: Dickhead alert! You could work that out from my log on time. Well, sent the text anyway kinda hoping you are going to come on here and that we can make it all better.

The Don: OK, so I've read every word and here comes my reply.

The Don: It makes me feel sad to see that I have caused this pain for you. I don't know if there is anything I can do to change things. You probably won't read this reply but I'll send you another text later to say that I'm leaving this on here until tomoz and then, if you've not been back, I'll take this chatroom down. I'll not text you anymore after that, if that's what you want.

The Don: I do not blame you for being angry with me. I can see that your past is much worse than mine. I know we began with just sex chat but it became a real friendship and I can see that what started as a helping relationship for both of us has changed. The only point I would challenge is that about therapy. I know you were hurt in therapy. I am being more lucky; my therapist challenges and supports me and I feel I am learning the things I need to right now. I write this next sentence to you as a compliment – you were the one who opened up the possibility of therapy for me and you should be proud to have been able to do that for another human being. Thank you my love.

The Don: I'm crying as I'm writing this all to you. I've got my headphones on and I'm listening to our song. My sweet Loulou, the pain is great right now. I am sorry that it seems that my gains in our relationship have been achieved selfishly.

The Don: I hope you only wrote the bits about prostituting yourself to hurt me – it does; please don't do that to yourself. I know you think I didn't hear you but I did. If the prostitution thing is about money for Amy, getting her to uni, I'LL HELP. I know you wouldn't accept any money from me but could you let me send you something for Amy.

The Don: I love the way she sounds, the way she still loves her mum and I think everyone should have a chance in life. I only wish I'd bought you a new car months back and given you a load of cash – it so hurts me to think you would sell your beautiful self for money (I know it's none of my business). The money's yours, just ask.

The Don: I could write a thousand words to you. I have just printed your poem and am going to frame it so that whatever happens between us now, I will be reminded of you. A piece of my heart it seems will be forever yours.

The Don: I had thought we would meet again soon – the hotel in Norfolk is all paid up. If you would like to use it, I can arrange it for you. Loulou, I hope this is not the end but if it is I DO understand why.

The Don: You are obviously not going to drop in here. As I said I'll send you another text – No pressure, but I'll just leave it 24 hours as I don't want you to come back here because you can't take the pressure of me keep writing to you.

The Don: Goodnight my sweetheart. Love you so very much and sorry to have caused you so much pain. If you contact JJ I only have myself to blame. If I need to I'll face it all up. I know I really should.

The Don: I wish I had a poem to send you. Mwwwhhhh xxxxxxxx I hope this is not goodbye but it is up to you. Really.

The Don: PS. If I do take the island down as you don't want us to continue I'll keep my SIM open for a month. Then if you change your mind I've not totally disappeared. Yes, I know you have my address and if you have JJ's mobile I expect you could find my real one but I trust you still. One month and then that would be that. I'll trust you really do want rid of me and I'll never bother you.

The Don: Nighty night sweet Loulou xxx sorry xxx.

11.48pm Louise is taking a break from the line. She turns to her computer and reads what Marc has written.

WELCOME TO THE ISLAND

Skippy: *Joined the chat*
Skippy: I need to leave you/us. I know you do as well.

Skippy: Book the Hotel in Norfolk for next weekend. No excuses. I want you there and I don't care what you have to do to sort it but be there. I'll be careful how I word this. There is NO blackmail in this but I'll take the money you OFFER for Amy and I won't contact JJ.

Skippy: This is what I want to happen Marc. Arrive, have coffee, go to our room, have sex, shower, dress for dinner and buy me the best meal they have on the menu. We then return to our room and fuck each other AND THEN YOU LEAVE. That's it then. The end. Almost. I like your idea of an open SIM for one month after the meeting – no contact by then, it's over, I'll never bother you again and I demand the same respect from you. Let me know that you've arranged it.

·•· ·•· ·•·

The Don: *from x.x.x63 cleared the room*

The Don: Understood, cleared the room. I'll meet you at the hotel 3.45 Saturday 27.

15 a lioness to the gates of hell

26 October 2007 (session 31)

'I think it's taken me quite a long time to come to terms with what she said.'

'You mean she challenged you?'

'Yeah. First I was shocked because I didn't see it coming like that. I'm embarrassed to say this here but I guess … I guess I had some idea that we'd do the work on the porn addiction, I'd sort something out with JJ and then, God I'm an arse … and then I could get it all sorted out with Louise.'

'Sort it out with Louise? How? In what way?' I ask Marc.

'I … I guess I feel stupid here now,' he displays a puzzled look on his face, 'exposed by, no, through my own selfish desires. I think I imagined having it all. I thought I'd meet with Louise once in a while, have sex with her, love her, but essentially nothing needed to change … God, I'm so self-centred.'

It's hard to argue with that right now, Marc.

'So you feel you realize a selfishness in yourself Marc. Is that a good or a bad thing to realize?'

His bottom lip curls, 'Well, it could be a good thing if I do something about it! I did … do love Lou you know, but she was right about me. I guess I didn't expect to find such truth from her.' He pauses. 'Fuck, how can I say that? I feel like I'm saying how could a woman have such insight into me. It seems I'm awash with truth right now. You know, I welcome what you've reflected to me, I can see it must be difficult to hold the mirror up to someone like me.'

I smile at him. Feeling slightly exposed myself at having internally agreed with his 'self-centred' comment, his sudden honesty in the room leads me to feel warm towards him. *He is making progress despite himself.*

'So, do you think we could go a little deeper with this honesty, Marc?'

'Do you have something in mind then?'

'Well, I'm aware that you might be willing to look at your part in all of this from more than one angle now.'

'In what way?' says Marc.

'Well, I wonder if we might look at the power you actually have. And we might see how this could be different for Louise and even Judy.'

'I'm intrigued; go on,' he says.

'Do you think you might be interested in looking at how this seems to be fitting together from a gender perspective?'

'Can I say "no"!' he smiles as he says it. I do not acknowledge the jest.

'Absolutely you can say "no".'

'I was joking,' he says. 'Really, just a joke … you know me.'

'Without wanting to be too "psychobabble" about it,' I say, 'for want of a better phrase, "many a true word spoken in jest?"'

Marc's facial expression flattens.

'Something's just come to mind,' he says. 'The one thing I learned from my father was "never spurn a woman". When I was in my early twenties and still thinking about carving out a life for myself in academia there was a big stink when my father had an affair with one of his female students. It wasn't too icky in the sense that it wasn't a young undergrad that he deflowered! She turned out to be a very attractive but mature PhD student. Nonetheless, you can imagine the many difficulties it caused in his faculty. You know the sort of thing – this woman was gaining privilege because she was shagging my father – the talk of impropriety and power were obvious blah, blah, blah.

'When it came to my father and mother it was awful.'

Intriguing that the mention of power and gender has finally brought your father into the room as more than a passing visitor.

'I think much of this might have been to do with the fact that it was only a few months after Ronny killed herself. I don't think my parents were at all close by then anyway. I think mother might have been as surprised as Simone and I were that my father still wanted to fuck someone. I didn't think he even had a cock he seemed that repressed!'

'And why does this come up now?' I enquire of the connection Marc is making in his own mind.

'Your talk of gender and power just made me remember that I actually thought more highly of him after it was discovered that he was shagging this woman – Siobhan. I thought more of him as a man when I knew he could still "pull"; that he was virile enough to get inside a younger woman's knickers.'

Silence.

'But this dalliance came to light in the December, and Ronny had committed suicide at the beginning of October. I still think … no …' Marc seems to change his mind as to what to say. 'It was horrid for him in particular … she slit her wrists in the bath. Her girlfriend found her in the water a few hours later. At first it seemed there was no note from her but two days later … my … my father received a note in the post from her. Apparently it said, "Why didn't you do something Papa."' Marc pauses. 'I don't know what he thought of it, I can't imagine how he must have felt but I know Simone and I both thought it meant she killed herself because she still couldn't live with all the childhood experiences she had been through … but we've never really spoken about it. I can remember murmurs that Ronny was unhappy about her sexuality – being a lesbian – but I never thought it was to do with that.

'Last week when I got that long message from Louise, her anger and hurt at me, I knew what to write back straight away – like my father was guiding me. His words to me came to mind. In an odd bonding moment after he had been caught with his hands down Siobhan's knickers, he said to me, "Never spurn a woman, for if you do, she will sit as a lioness to the gates of hell."'

'You remember his exact words?'

'No, that's my translation of what he said – we only ever spoke in French unless we were in company.'

There is a tearful feeling in the room; something like poetry and pain hang in the space for a moment. My mind makes a connection to the BDSM activities Marc has often spoken about to me. Although I'd like to work with the connection, other things seem more relevant.

Silence.

'I swore then to myself that I'd not be as stupid as he had been. I remember thinking how affairs were for lonely, stupid men. The irony is too great for me right now.'

Silence.

'It seems that the mention of masculine power has brought a lot up in the room, Marc.'

'Ha, yes. But I'm really interested in what you were digging about for.'

'It's in rather a different vein. You'd been challenging yourself to look in the mirror. But now, things have rather shifted with the stuff about Ronny and your father. I'm not certain an intellectual process would fit very well with the rather raw emotions that feel alive in the room. I'm also aware that it's the first time your father has been so centre stage. He always seems to have had a walk-on part and now that's changed.'

'I don't know how you manage this as a job, so much stuff creeping out of every conversation. I guess it's strange to look back twenty-odd years to find my father. "A walk-on part" you say. Well, yes, that was him. And now, again I feel embarrassed to say, he grew in my eyes because he was having it off with someone other than my mother.'

'Stay with the thought. What comes to mind?'

'I like the idea that he put the boot into my mother. I don't know whether to laugh, cry or cheer him for that. Someone at my father's college tipped my mother off in a phone call. Some stiff uptight bitch spoiled my father's fun.'

Are we really talking about your father or is this some parallel process to your own loss of an affair with Louise? 'Bitch' you call her? Well, that could also be about Louise phoning Judy? Difficult that I dislike your mother so much that I can't challenge 'spoiled my father's fun' … of course I can. Don't want to just yet though do I? Follow him.

'It's a very strange image that comes to mind.'

'For sharing in the space?'

'I knew Siobhan a little,' says Marc. 'I guess my father was a devil really. A few times when I was down from Cambridge she was at the house working on some "project" with him. I can imagine the sort of project they were working on!' he laughs. 'My father introduced us directly, no shame whatsoever. She was around thirty-four, thirty-five. Brunette, full, kissable lips. A nice round arse, you know the sort of thing – very fuckable.'

Asking me to collude with your image of women again.

'And the image that came to mind?'

'Once I'd heard that they had been shagging each other I actually fantasized a few times about walking into my father's study at home. I always pictured them rutting on the desk. I was pleased to see my father fucking Siobhan. The pleasure was a sort of sadistic one. In my head, behind me, my mother would walk in and the shock would kill her stone dead.'

Silence.

'Your mother killed by the sight of her husband having sex with a much younger woman – the desk like an alter, some sort of sacrifice?' I ask.

'God, yes! But not sacrifice. My mother slaughtered by the potent masculine power that it turned out the repressed Camille had been secretly building behind her back.'

Good analysis, Marc.

'The triumph of your father over your mother.'

'Poor Ronny …'

Silence.

'Why poor Ronny then?'

'Me finding the good father,' he says, 'the strong father who could slay the evil mother. It was father as … as our … our protector – fuck my bitch mother!'

Silence.

'It seems to me, Marc, that there might be some real connection with all this and the "Island" entry that Louise wrote? Perhaps we *should* look at the power relationship between you?'

'How do you mean?'

'Well, you say that your father went up in your estimation by having sex with another woman. So much so that you even fantasized that you were there at the moment of his discovery and the subsequent death of your mother – this is powerful "life force" stuff. Omnipotent power. You seem to enjoy the fact that the sex makes your father strong enough to defend you by killing your mother essentially through the act itself. It leaves me with an interpretation to offer in the form of a question: "Why do you cast Judy as your mother?"'

'I don't follow the question?'

'In having the affair with Louise, in using porn how you do, you seem to be identifying with your father. What does that gain you in the context you have just been talking about your father in?'

Marc is motionless as he thinks. 'Strength, virility?'

'And in claiming strength and virility in this way do you not cast Judy as the to-be "destroyed woman"? Do you not cast Judy as your mother against the "fatal" masculine façade?'

'But I love Judy.'

'You love Judy?'

'Yes, I do … isn't it possible to love two people at the same time?'

'Do you think you love Louise?'

'Do you think I don't?'

'*That's* not really my question Marc.'

'I think I do in a particular sort of way.'

'So how do you show this love towards these women?'

'I provide a lifestyle for Judy – the house …'

I interrupt Marc. 'But she is your equal; you've said Judy earns as much as you do.'

Silence.

'Not splitting hairs with you but a bigger part of that house is mine through my inheritances and I protected Louise from herself those times we met – you said.'

'Yes, a few times in her life, but are you doing that for Louise now? Can she "build" from what you offer her?'

I wonder if that is a fair question. Transferentially, I wonder how much *I'd* like to protect Louise.

Marc switches back to talking about Judy.

'I love Judy – look how many years we have been together.'

'Have you?'

'Have I what?' he questions, slightly rattled.

'Really been together? You complain that Judy is not there for you but are you there for her? And are you there for Louise? Remember Mrs Smith and Mr Jones?'

This is a disorientating session. I'm concerned I'm off the mark with my lines of enquiry and questions. And yet there is something I'm picking up. It is that familiar feeling Marc broadcasts when he is holding something back. But today I'm still a little lost in the flow of things. I look at him across the room. His eyes are reddening. I know that I am walking a tightrope. On one side lies possible movement, a breakthrough in self-insight. On the other, perhaps a therapy that breaks down. *Maybe I've mistimed this push.*

'Remind me,' he says.

'Mrs Smith is happily married; she has two children, a happy social life, a fulfilling job. Mr Jones is single, lonely, with hardly a friend in the world.'

'Ah yes I remember them.'

'And so you remember that they both have only 100 "energy" points to spend each day. Mr Jones would talk and make a friend of Mrs Smith if only she would stand that bit longer on the corner during the dog walks they meet each other on. Mr Jones always has plenty of spare energy points to spend. Mrs Smith, however, can't "afford" to spend too many with Mr Jones, as she has lots of people that need her energy points – but she is always careful to save a few for Mr Smith at the end of the day.'

Impatiently Marc says, 'Yes, I remember how the whole scenario goes.'

'So how many points do you spend on porn, how many on Louise, how many do you have left for Judy at the end of the day?'

Silence.

'But you're not showing me how to escape all this yet … it's simple for you and you make out as if it's simple for me. How do you expect me to change just like that?'

Silence.

'Interesting phrase Marc, "you're not showing me how to escape". I'm not certain how to respond in one sense as it's the first time in all our work you seem to have made explicit that sort of mindset.'

'Mindset?'

'You make it sound as if *I* am supposed to change you rather than walk alongside you as *you* engage in *your own* change process.'

'There you go again; it's okay over there, it's fine from your chair. You have the answers, you don't have to do the work!'

Okay, big negative transference here, follow him in – stay in the here-and-now. It's the right track after all.

'Are you asking me to feel sorry for you?'

'Uhh?' Marc displays a pained face like a toddler losing his comforter. 'What does that mean?'

'What is it you don't understand here?'

'Any of it!' raising his voice a little, 'I don't fucking understand any of it, everyone's calling for something different!'

'So you are experiencing this part of our work as me asking you to do something?'

'Oh, no. You're too clever for that,' he says bitingly.

'So you are feeling angry towards me, Marc?'

Silence.

A gentle voice, almost a whisper, says, 'I can't do this!'

Silence.

What's the 'this'? What can't you do, Marc? 'This' in the room or 'this' with Louise or some other 'this'? Come on!

'You can't do this?' I respond gently and then echoing his whisper, 'This?'

'I promised myself that I wouldn't fall into this trap again in these sessions …'

I am genuinely puzzled for a moment. Again, what can't I see?

'… okay, so there was more chat with Louise last week on the

Island. You're going to think this is a really bad idea – I wanted to talk about it on Monday.'

Ah, the hidden stuff and judgement; he thinks I'm going to judge him. Let's get this in quickly so as to smooth the way.

'You think I am going to judge you for something, Marc?'

Silence.

'Well, I don't see how you can't – sorry for getting uptight just now.'

'There's nothing to apologize for Marc,' I reply.

'Later on, Louise left me another message. She said that she wanted to meet at the hotel in Norfolk on Saturday – tomorrow; that she would accept the money I offered her for Amy and that, after that, if a month passes and we've not made contact with each other it's really over.'

'You haven't mentioned money before, Marc.'

'I was feeling very bad,' Marc says. 'She seems to be totally broke. I couldn't stand it and I knew she wouldn't accept anything from me.'

'So you were surprised when she accepted it?'

'Well, you've got to agree that if I offered her the money it would make her seem like a prostitute in the end call.'

'I can certainly see how that might come across – but the money for her daughter?'

'Yes, money to get her to university next year – guess it's Lou's sort of dream.'

'I wonder if Amy wants it?' I say.

'By all accounts she's really very bright, she has a place at Oxford, so I guess it feels good to help her as much as Lou – everyone deserves a chance don't they? … So that's it. What do you think?'

I hadn't expected a direct question. I stall for time to think, 'I wonder why you ask me that as a direct question Marc?'

'Because I'm interested how you are "not going to judge me",' he says rather sarcastically.

I smile at the dig, 'That sounds rather a taunt towards me, Marc. Are you trying to box me in? Are you angry at me or yourself?'

'How come when I decide to be honest, I can't get an honest reply?'

I smile again, 'I think you know the answer to that.'

'Oh really?'

'Yes, really. But I'm happy to give you that reply if you really want it.'

I play my card calculating that he will not want my response now there has been a challenge.

Silence.

Again with a hint of sarcasm he says, 'Perhaps we should talk about therapist power.'

'I can only do one thing at a time,' I say, taking care to be gentle in my response. 'Which would you like me to engage with? A conversation about how you experience power in the consulting room or the answer to the question you asked about judgement?'

Silence.

'I'm interested in what you might say about my situation, my choice.'

I give a therapeutically defensible answer, 'Well, it seems to me that you are angry with yourself and you are projecting this anger into me. You'd like me to tell you what to do; perhaps you'd like me to tell you off, to tell you not to go tomorrow? Perhaps you'd like me to tell you that you are a fool for giving Louise money, that yes, it makes her your prostitute, that she is in a weak position and must succumb to your power in the form of cash and that there is, by any other name, blackmail involved in her bargain with you. I notice that you have not told me how much money you are giving her. A hundred pounds? Perhaps a thousand? I don't know but I expect you feel uncertain that it's the right thing to do. But you don't need me to tell you any of these things as you already know them very well.'

Silence.

Marc wriggles in his chair and then very quietly says: 'It's eight thousand pounds.'

Shit, eight grand! What's my responsibility here? Shit, why did you tell me that – eight grand's a lot of money? Do you really know what you're doing, Marc? Shit, I wish I could get this to supervision before you give Louise the money.

Silence.

'That's a great deal of money Marc; I'm quite concerned about this.'

'So you *are* going to judge me!'

'No. I want you to know how concerned I am that you might not be fully able to see what is going on here. I think you are rather vulnerable, the power is perhaps not with you at all and I underline the fact that blackmail by Louise seems a possibility.'

'I've thought of that but I see I've run out of time today,' Marc says.

I note how stuck I feel myself. He is right; we have already run over by a couple of minutes. Marc leaves no option to offer him an extension to the session as he stands up, and by the time I am out of my chair he already has his hand on the door handle. He does not stop for us to perform our usual parting ritual. He is on the terrace already. He looks back at me and waves a hand.

'See you Monday,' he calls.

'Yes Marc.' *Be careful; don't do anything you will regret.* 'See you Monday.'

16 don't go cold turkey

'So things have been much more intense inside you? Is that what you are saying?'

'Yes, it's like it was before I started coming to see you. What was it you called it? "My habit, my analgesic."'

I'm certain the reason Marc is feeling like this and is using pornography so heavily at the moment is because he has not been in touch with, nor had contact from, Louise. *I think you love to play 'hide and surprise'. Not a mention of her in the last few weeks; even with the prompts and the direct questions, you've dodged bringing her into the room.*

'So, you know why you are using porn so much right now, don't you?' I say.

'It's just like an energy inside me, I can't find another way to shift it. Does that make any sense to you?'

'A little,' I reply, 'but let me ask you almost the same question again: why do you think your use of porn has suddenly risen after a period when you were reporting to me that you were making good progress?'

Marc shifts about in his chair and pours a glass of water. I feel impatient for a moment. *The longer you leave me waiting, the less certain I am about whether you've had contact with Louise or not. God, I think I'm missing her. Is that in the transference or did I really build such a strong picture of her myself? Come on, you know it's because you wish you could have worked with both of them – couples therapy with Marc and Louise; that would have been a learning curve. Concentrate now – take that thought to supervision. Perhaps it's that he's in conflict with himself, that he's missed the chance to break away from Louise, that using porn is a defence against this.*

Marc puts his hands out, palms up gesturing: you help me; I don't know.

'Louise?' I say.

He clears his throat; he is uncomfortable. 'Yes, Louise.'

Silence.

'So?' I gesture back the same action: you help me; I don't know.

Marc's head falls. He rests it in his hands. He parts his middle and index fingers so that he forms a mask over his mouth and nose with his other fingers. It accentuates his eyes and amplifies his breath. He looks depressed, alone, tortured even.

Ah, hide and surprise – here we go, pure Marc.

'All I can think of when I've spent a lot of time on the web is Mrs Smith and Mr Jones. That story has really stayed in my mind. It means a lot.' Marc pauses. 'I've … I've not spent a minute actually connected to Louise. There has not been one text, not one call from her since we met in Norfolk. My gap with her has been total; I know I've avoided every one of your enquiries about her. I wouldn't be surprised if you thought I'd carried on talking to her but … but the truth is … the truth is she has simply walked away.' He closes the v-shape made by his fingers and completes the mask over his face.

I listen to Marc's irregular breathing patterns. The short, sorrowful noise of his internal happenings, the percussive intakes of this middle-aged man crying with genuine woe.

That's not what I expected. The lead up – thought there was about to be a Marc bombshell at the other end, not such emotion from within. You really are desolate, empty … no, abandoned; that's it, abandoned.

Five minutes pass before Marc is ready to talk again. With a sigh he begins a sentence. 'How many times have I said this sort of thing to you in this space – you know,' he sighs once more, 'the other night I sank to new depths. Totally uninterested in sex, just like the times when Lou made me feel really angry.'

Silence.

Marc needs a prompt.

'You say "new depths". Do you want to bring them?'

Seems I was right the first time – so there is a Marc surprise in waiting.

'You already know what I did in a way … I end up turning to ever-more gross sexual stuff.'

'Do you know what you were trying to do in turning to porn like this?'

'To finally "wake me up",' he motions air quotes, his favourite action when talking like this, 'and "get me off". What in the fuck am I looking at a Croatian women having sex with a horse and then getting fucked by a dog for? It's not got anything to do with sex, just humiliation and degra-dation. I feel so fucking stuffed up, stale, dirty. I feel like some great ulcer has burst inside me and I'm full of and swimming in the pus.'

No lead-up to the zoophilia, just shock and awe – new style Marc; let's reflect that style back to you, no place to rest for a moment.

I do not let the room fall to silence but follow straight on from Marc's words. 'It seems to me that perhaps there is a chance for you to turn yourself around right now.'

'Now? Why?'

'Louise is absent.'

'I'm not certain I follow?'

'My feeling is that all the time you were with her you had locked yourself out from really acting or doing anything with the Mrs Smith and Mr Jones story – despite the fact that you say the idea has stayed with you. What do you really want from this process, Marc?'

'I really have to stop this stuff once and for all. I'm always at the extreme end, pushing the boundary, aren't I?'

'I agree with you Marc. I remember at the beginning of our work you told me the net was like the free sweet shop and that if someone didn't stop they would get rotten teeth, get sick and die, something like that, so what *do* you want? What do you *really* want?' My tone is firm. This is a big challenge. A challenge I've been expecting to make. *If you don't want to heal yourself now, I'm afraid for you. Perhaps this just isn't the right time to do this work; shit that's a depressing thought now we've come this far. Don't you want to deal with the pain you are in, how this all links to porn, where it comes from so you can be free? Not just digging up unrelated events from the past – what have we been doing for the last forty sessions, Marc?*

Silence.

'I'd love to get back to looking at a pretty woman in a magazine and that being the turn on. You know, looking at the shape of her breasts the curve of her bum. Enjoying the nakedness, the beauty of the subject, not jerking to the degradation and objectification. I really do need your help with this – tell me what to do.'

There is hope. We can deal with the detail later. The beauty of the subject: degradation and objectification of women – that would make a good aesthetics paper within the field of art or pornography!

'Okay, Marc. I hear you. You want out of the porn trap but you still seem to think I'll do it for you …'

Marc interrupts me, 'Sorry, I should have said, help me find out what I have to do.'

I smile at him. 'Certainly Marc.'

We sit in silence in the room. There is a glow. Almost a sense of peace. My breath passes easily from my lungs. Despite the 'depraved' nature of the zoophilia Marc has just spoken about, there is a different feeling. The sense that he is always about to disclose evermore 'revolting', 'humiliating' and 'disgusting' thoughts, fantasies and experiences seems suddenly absent.

'You know Marc,' I say almost in a whisper, as if fearful of breaking the 'spell' that is alive in the room, 'you already have in place so many of the tools you need to recover. You are perhaps fully cognisant of the pain you endured during your early life. You know that you are masochistic in your use of the Internet – it is the very thing you cling to and for want of a better phrase torture yourself with, but still you use it. You have grossed yourself out with zoophilia.'

He interrupts again, 'I know, I know. Fuck, fuck, fuck!'

'Let me ask you a very similar question for a third time today: what do you want from this process?'

'I want to be in control of myself, I want to feel happy, easy with myself and I don't want to go behind JJ's back any more. I don't know, perhaps I even have to tell her about everything.'

'I think that's the first time you've ever brought Judy up in that way – really acknowledging that she is in the dark, that your activities are clandestine. They're secrets from her.'

'I really do love her. None of this is fair on her. I can only imagine how I would feel if it was her acting like this and I found out about it. But where do I start? Where? Point me in the right direction.'

I smile and pause before I speak. 'Marc, you began this process forty sessions ago. It seems to me that you've just become free of Louise but that there were deeply personal things you had invested in her that you really want to be invested with Judy. There are things you have so far only told Louise and things you have only told me – things about the scars your childhood has left you with. It seems to me the question is not "Where do I start?" but "How do I continue? What do I do next?"' Again I smile at him.

Silence.

No angry fire back at me, no sidestep Marc?

Marc smiles at me. His face says continue.

'Let me reiterate the first principles of our work. You are desensitized to many sexual acts and to your sexual feelings and fantasies. You have also lost your, for want of a better term, "moral control". I am here as your intelligent mirror, to reflect to you that you've lost your way more than a little here. Do one of two things until I see you next. Limit yourself to one Internet site or decide not to visit a site at all.'

'I'm not going back on the Internet for sex.'

'Fine. But just like people on a diet, the moment they say "I'm not eating chocolate", they crave it. You can't ban yourself from all porn and just go "cold turkey". My experience in this room with men and women addicted to different aspects of pornography and cybersex relationships tells me that does not work. There is a sense of loss to be worked through here. Louise, the Internet, to name two. Louise was a real human being, a real interaction; let's separate the two out. Our work with her will emerge as we go on. But the Internet has been doing all your fantasy work for you. Do you remember how I spoke about this when we first met?'

Marc nods, 'Yes, you suggested that I'd probably stopped using my own creative imagination around sex.'

'And?' I ask.

'It's very subtle … but I think you're right.'

'You didn't really notice when you switched over from masturbatory fantasy that was creative to either replaying clips you'd seen on the net or simply having a masturbatory drive that made you turn to your laptop, unzip and surf!'

There is a slight smirk between us at my final phrase – it feels affirming of the therapeutic alliance.

'Yes, I don't use my sexual imagination any more, you're right. If I do open a magazine then it seems to take me so long to get interested that I simply move on to the web. I don't even really look at DVDs any more. It's quicker and easier to flick the laptop open – there's a full range to fit any mood right there in front of you. The process really has been that subtle that until you mentioned it, it was completely hidden to me.'

'I'm just looking at the clock and notice we are all but done. A few days Marc, see what you can do. Take control. Do it for yourself and perhaps for Judy and you as a couple.'

'But don't go "cold turkey", yeah?'

'When you need some relief, go back a step, turn to an older habit; it will still be there – "healthier" in relative terms; try a DVD or perhaps you could even buy a magazine, something you have to put some effort into. It might not be where you want to end up, but you really do have to break the power of the net first of all. If you are going to begin to resensitize yourself Marc, we need to reverse our steps, go back to where you came in.

'It seems simple in here. It's safe, perhaps this is a place porn can't get in.'

'Are you saying you're scared?'

'Sort of. What do I do if I can't get off without the Internet?'

'Why don't you try and see?'

'Is this going to work?'

Can I be congruent here? Give him hope but not lies. Say what you believe in the here-and-now. 'I think you can do it because I believe what you are telling me – that you want to stop; that you want to like, even love, yourself; that there is understanding and care for yourself available not only here but within you; and that perhaps you are even hungry to find that care and understanding in your marriage. I think you can do this now. Step by step, free yourself and get your life back.'

'See you Monday?'

'Yes Marc, I'll see you on Monday.'

17 back to bettie

'As I've said before, therapy is a place to visit, not live. I think you're right: it might not be quite the right time to drop to one session a week, but it really does seem like it's not that far away.'

'That means a lot to me.'

'Why's that?' I enquire gently.

'Well, if you think I might be able to get by on one session a week it feels like I really must have made some progress.'

'If you want to take that from it then yes, why not look at it that way. But remember, I'm just that intelligent mirror; I reflect back to you what you broadcast to me. I remind you that there's no point in telling yourself a lie.' I smile and Marc smiles back. *There really has been an incredible change in you over the last two months – the rewards of this job can be great.*

'I don't know why I've waited this far into the session to tell you this, but you know me! When I was out there doing it I wanted to phone you up and tell you how I'd coped; I was proud I guess.'

Intrigued by the 'proud' statement, I gesture 'tell me' before saying, 'I'm listening if you want to talk about it.'

'It's odd … I feel kind of odd about it. For me this was a really good thing, yet I'm aware that perhaps it was part of how I got to my really dark place. Still, I know you keep reminding me that this is all about resensitization, that we are going "backwards" towards our goal.'

'In reverse perhaps, rather than backwards?'

'Sure, in reverse. Well, it's been fifty-two days – inclusive – since I last used the net for looking at porn. It's not that I'm counting up every day … it's just that I counted up on Wednesday because I was feeling tempted by the net. Work was stressful, this bloody reorganization of the staff groups I'm doing – you remember, I was telling you about it last session. I realized that I was feeling tempted. Stress was leading to a desire to tune out with porn but I sort of switched off to it, reminded myself of the task I was trying to achieve, reminded myself that all I have to do is keep away from porn on the net; that this is my choice. But as I began to drive home I just had all this stuff going around in my mind. I was thinking about how I could go home and just use my mobile for a quick sex chat to avoid the net. It was unconscious almost and then … and then I thought how fucking annoyed I was that I'd exchange one drug for another and that even though I'd cut up the sex SIM card, I was willing to start using my main mobile for sex chat. I turned left into Green End Road instead of right into King's Hedges; there's a little lay-by on the left a few yards down. I pulled into it and phoned my mobile company, asked them to bar premium rate calls from my phone.

'You know, it was quite difficult to get them to do it. "You do realize you won't be able to use this such-and-such service …" on and on they went. Anyway, long story short, the mobile was blocked then and there while I sat in that lay-by. But the fucking Internet, you know blah, blah, blah. All I could think of was it sitting at home waiting for me. I phoned JJ, told her I loved her, told her how we should get our act together tonight when she got home and have a meal out. She loved the idea; I said I'd book our favourite place. I sat there in that lay-by. I sat there and booked the table. I had thoughts of how JJ and I might get it on when we got home. I had myself feeling horny for my wife; you don't know how good that made me feel. She seemed to want *me* … I wanted her right then. But still, the Internet was sitting there in my mind. In fact, I think it felt worse. In my mind, I was throwing up pictures of JJ and then Louise kept creeping in. Both their faces in my mind, both of their ecstasy expressions imprinted in my mind. I knew if I just drove straight home I'd be on the Internet. I counted in my diary. It was … it's like … amazing I counted forty-seven days without a single peep at anything even slightly smutty let alone porn. I thought of you, the space, the work we've done here. Yet, at the same time it was like forty-seven rolled round to fifty and began flashing in my mind as a neon sign; fifty, it's a time for celebration! I so nearly started the car up and drove home. So nearly I went home to celebrate fifty days clear of net porn by going onto the net to prove I could have just one look. But then your reminder, your words were in my head. All the stuff about "reverse". I knew what to do. I drove to a newsagent that's just down the road. It used to be one of my favourite newsagents to buy mags from. I went into the newsagent and did what I used to do years ago. I looked along the top shelf, well, top two shelves they have so much! All the mags were still there: *Fiesta*, *Mayfair*, *Escort* but also all the harder imports as well. I reached down and picked up a copy of a newspaper and at the same time a copy of an import. I've always wondered what it is with those US mags. I picked up the November issue in January yet it was actually on the newsstands in September, sorry, blah blah blah. Anyway, I was full of adrenaline. Really, quite shaky. And you know what … it felt great; I was excited in an old-fashioned way … like I used to be as a teenager. I sat in the car after I'd bought the magazine. Flicked through the pages. It's the way I used to sort of "charge myself up". I'd flick through and get a few images going in my head so that by the time I got home I'd be ready for a fast, furious wank. The mag was a good one. Lesbian strap-on, a nice dildo spread with a big-titted blonde, at the back there was a pretty steamy three-way – two girls one bloke – doing stuff with toys and finger penetration, but what caught my eye most were some stills from a video with two of my favourite brunettes, Primavera and Adelynn Girard. Adelynn had this huge black dildo in her pussy and was about to push another one into Primavera's arse, I tell you.' Marc stops suddenly. Then he continues, 'I sound like a salesman for the porn industry – God knows why I'm giving you all this detail. I bought a porn mag instead of using the Internet. I had a meal, impromptu, with my wife. I felt alive for a while. I wanted to make love to my wife. We did, and I didn't take two hours getting myself there. Full stop.'

Marc had spoken as if in one breath for more than six minutes. Although buying an imported, hardcore, pornographic magazine from a newsagent might sound like a failure to heal his difficulties, it is, in fact, a step towards resensitization. The hyper feelings he was reporting, the searching for a connection with Judy and the action to disengage with his phone and the Internet, appeared, in my consulting room, to be an engagement with life. The purchase of the pornographic magazine became an active retrograde step, not a passive, desensitized act.

I smile as I begin to talk, 'Well, this sounds like a very encouraging development. Let's just break it down into all the component parts and see what we can glean from this, shall we? First, it's good to hear that it's been so long already since you last used the Internet to look at porn. You were aware of feeling stressed with the work situation and importantly you became aware that the porn thoughts were your disguised craving for an analgesic for the stress you were feeling. You managed to remain focused on the task, at least until you finished work. Once you were on your own in the car you realized in fact how tempted you were, how hyper-aroused you were feeling, and what you ended up doing was supporting yourself in the task you are trying to achieve by having the premium mobile calls barred. To be honest, I thought I had suggested that to you myself a long time ago.'

'Actually you did; I just thought I could do it without taking that step.'

'Well even better, you took control when you needed to rather than following an "instruction". The important thing is you felt able to do it. You then invested your energy in the most important thing: Judy. You got an intimate reward from her; you felt she wanted you and you felt connected to her. Impressively, you also managed to get a sexual buzz from, about, your wife. Then you continued to realize that you were still under threat. The Internet was the thing you most wanted to avoid; the pull of the addiction was great. Okay, so then you substituted one type of hardcore pornography with another, but for our journey, the most important thing is that you have continued to break the link to the net and the "free sweet shop". You were never "addicted" to magazines as you are to the net. In fact, I'm not certain it's possible to be addicted to magazines in the way you are to the net.'

'So do you think I did the right thing? It felt good to me but I'm not the expert.'

'The expert thing again: how many times have we …?'

Marc laughs out loud, a hearty sound crackling in the air; it breaks the spell of the secretness of the acts he's been talking about. The sound ricochets around the walls, becoming infectious as it continues. My face finally cracks. This is an important part of who Marc is, his charm, the way in which he attempts to make me collude with him.

As if we were informally thrown together in the room, Marc pushes some words out. 'Sorry… I don't know why … why … that's so funny to me … I think there was just … just a look on your face.' He begins to calm. 'There was this look on your face that was in such contrast to the material we were talking about … it was like … sorry … sorry … it was like all this stuff I bring in to the room, you never do anything but take it in. I don't think I've ever seen you wince, look uneasy with all the *merde* I bring in, you don't judge all this awful stuff … but if I call you the expert, the one who knows, you start to put out all these feelings and looks … I'm sorry. And I do know what you mean, you really don't have to repeat the stuff about power in the room, equality, knowledge … it's just difficult to remember sometimes.'

I'm a touch perplexed, a touch self-conscious about my expressions.

'Well, I don't know what expression I'm showing now, and to be honest I've lost my way with that laughter. God knows what *I've* been laughing at but as a wise supervisor once said to me: "It's okay to get lost sometimes." Okay … yes … we were finishing looking at the process you'd gone through the other night. Shall I finish up what I was going to say?'

'Please do. I'm sorry, being like that.'

I smile. 'To be honest, really congruent to what I was going to say, I think I'm going to be contradictory. I think I was actually going to be a sort of expert for a second; I was going to offer one detail to you, one thing that could have perhaps,' I motion air quotes, as if reflecting Marc's own style to him for a moment, '"improved".'

'I'm not going to make you run away from it am I?' says Marc.

'Perhaps if you had bought a copy of *Mayfair* or *Escort* it would have been an even bigger step, something softcore, almost down to the erotic rather than the pornographic.'

'Yes, I agree. I thought the same – but I'm still impressed with myself.'

'And so you don't need my stamp of approval; the question you asked a while back was not really needed. Indeed, what you did, from where I sit, was almost textbook resensitization work.'

'Thank you.'

'Thank who?'

'Thank us both?'

'Sure, if that's how it feels, but praising yourself is the most important thing. It reminds you that you are in control.'

'Since I bought that mag it's reminded me how I used to use porn before the Internet. You just said that perhaps it's impossible to use magazines in the same way as the net, but I actually wonder if that's true? Having a new mag in the house has been interesting. I'd got rid of all my printed stuff – even the extreme hardcore pictures I had – not that long before I started coming here. Bringing that US mag into the house reminded me what an addict I am. I find myself sneaking a peek at it in the same way as I do the net. No, that's not quite true, it's not random sexual shocks like using the web; it's more like the "compulsive looking" side of the Internet. Perhaps in that particular mag it was because of Adelynn Girard. She has that Bettie Page-style fringe in it. I guess I'm obsessing on her. But thinking about it here you know it's a relief all the same. You're right that it's not pulling me further in like the net always makes you do. It *is* going in reverse, like you say. I used to compulsively look at magazine pictures and Bettie's right there near to my beginning with porn. She must have been the first woman I ever saw in bondage pictures. Black and whites of Bettie are even the only images on my computer – the only stuff actually stored on my hard drive. This is the stuff I got into everything else from, so yes, I am going in reverse. Adelynn Girard is just an echo of that … yes … I like it …'

'And importantly, although you are feeling obsessive, you are using it to build fantasies about Adelynn Girard, what you would like to do, watch, get involved with at a fantasy level. She reminds you of Bettie Page and I seem to remember you said that Judy looks a little like Bettie – she has the fringe and the same dark brunette colouring, so …?'

'I want … I want to be with JJ? I want JJ like this?'

'It might ask questions about what you really want from your sex life – the one that is real, loving, connected to a person who, throughout all this, you have said you love. The rest is fantasy; perhaps things you never dare talk about or ask for from the person you love. So we return to my often-repeated questions to you: What do you want?, Where do you want to get to?'

'Perhaps I can't give a single answer to that. Perhaps I have to let that develop. I think that's what we are getting to. I get the point: I don't need your permission, praise, whatever. I need to be comfortable with where I am and I can honestly say I feel more in touch with myself and alive by stopping my use of the net. Judy's around more now as this job of hers starts to close down, so it's good timing. By the end of the financial year she won't have any travel outside the UK and it will only be a few days a month that she is further away than the city, so … this all comes at a good time.'

Marc looks at the clock at just the same time as I do. 'That seems a good place to finish I think,' he says. 'Usual time on Friday?'

'Absolutely,' I reply.

PART THREE

9.38am Louise is lying on cold, broken Victorian terracotta tiles. They lead up to the house that she has just exited. Sprawled on the pathway, she is clearly in a great deal of pain. Virtually bare to the waist, her right arm is through the sleeve of what now looks like a tattered remnant. It was once her favourite black satin blouse. It was once the blouse Marc adored seeing her in. It is the blouse she was wearing the first day they met and the blouse she removed as they began to make love that first time. Now, her left breast hangs loose from it like an udder. If you were to look closely you would see scars on it from long ago, scars from abuse this part of her body has experienced; you would see that the marks were caused by burning the skin. Louise is in pain; she is bleeding from lesions in her anus and her vagina. She is aware for a moment of a warm spot near to her hip. It is the bundle of clothes she swept up in her hand as she half ran, was half thrown out of the tattered black door. It registers somewhere inside her that someone is looking at her over the garden gate, but she does not care; she is not really lying on the path, she is not really anywhere right now.

•◆• •◆• •◆•

For some time after Louise split up with Marc she felt there was a sense of empowerment in having left him. She felt almost pleased to notice that she had not been taken in too deeply by her own fantasies. She knew that there would never have been a way in which Marc and her could be together. A few times after the first month of their separation Louise called Judy's mobile phone. She did not know why she was doing it – not really.

'Hello, Judy Moreau,' Judy's voice sounds almost magical to Louise's ears – well spoken without being posh, light without being girly.

'Oh sorry, who is that?'

'Judy Moreau; can I help you?'

Can you help me? Oh yes, you can help me and I can help you too.

'I'm sorry, I think I must have the wrong number.'

'Okay, well I hope you get the right person next time. Goodbye.'

Not much chance of ever getting the right person for me, love. Fuck, why did you have to sound so nice, bitch?

The last time Louise called Judy she hooked up her phone to the minidisc recorder she uses when she wants to make a recording of a conversation she has with a punter on the chatline. Louise has kept lots of recordings of Marc when he used to phone her on that line and now, by spinning the beautifully polite Judy a line or two, she has the trophy of a short passage of dialogue with her to add to her collection.

Louise transfers all her minidisc conversations to her computer and then sometimes to CDs. The recordings she feels most turned on by make it onto her MP3 player. They become 'the partners' there is no risk of being rejected by. These are the voice she takes to bed, as they can never leave her. With the little white headphones stuck tightly into her ears she pulls up her bedclothes and drowns herself in an ecstasy of thoughts, words and intimate personal massage.

For a short period of time after Louise made her recording of Judy she placed it directly after her favourite conversation with Marc. She imagined that Judy would be lying beside her in the bed as Marc whispered in her ear. As Louise listens to Marc describe the sexual acts he wants to perform on her she imagines moving closer to Judy's cheek, their warm flesh touching as the two of them listen to his masturbatory vocal track together. While Marc's captured voice talks in Louise's headphones, she fantasizes that Judy's hand masturbates her. As the vocal track changes from Marc to Judy's voice, Louise is amazed how easy it is to bring herself to orgasm. Each time she climaxes like this Louise experiences it as a blissful revenge on Marc.

With more than a year and a half having passed since Louise and Marc last met she feels easier about having all but blackmailed him out of the £8,000 he had paid her. She realizes that despite the fact there had been a pretence between them both – that this money was for Amy – Louise knows it had really been the pay-off of herself as Marc's *'fille de joie'*. Many times she has thought back to how it felt when she picked up the plain brown envelope filled with £50 notes. She remembers they had just had farewell sex – first in the shower, then on the bed. Every time Marc began to lose his erection she would dismount him and suck him back to life. When that failed, she seemed to be able to threaten him into action. As he began to build to orgasm she prodded him over the edge by stimulating his prostate with her index finger.

When most of the country is restfully sleeping Louise is awake. At these times, between her punters' telephone calls she turns back to Marc and that final coupling. It was different. She thought she was aware that, perhaps, a dislike of her had already built up in him. She thought she sensed his fear of her and she became excited, very excited, by the power that was fleetingly bestowed upon her. She thought how, if the world was different, Marc would claim she raped him.

·◆· ·◆· ·◆·

When Louise had left the house the previous morning she had given Amy £100 cash and told her not to worry if she didn't return until Sunday evening.

Amy kissed her mother. 'I really love you mum,' she said.

'That's just the £100 speaking,' Louise replied.

'I'll probably not be back until late Sunday myself,' Amy said. 'Where you going mum?'

'I'm staying over at Dec's.'

'Oh mum! Do you know what you're doing with him? He's not really that kind to you if you ask me.'

Louise leans forward towards Amy; she kisses her on the centre of the forehead. 'Well I'm not asking you little madam.'

'He doesn't get a prize from me!'

Louise's eyes are filled with tears; she already knows inside that her daughter is right; she kisses her little girl again. 'How did you get to be so grown up? So smart? Nineteen years old and yet it seems like only yesterday I was wrapping you up for your first day at school. You didn't give me advice about men then – who's going to look after me when you go to university?'

'I'll be back to see you every weekend mum – don't you worry.'

'You won't have to bother with all that. You'll have your own life to lead when you get up to Oxford,' Louise says turning away.

Louise had not really wanted to talk to Amy this morning. She was looking forward to some time alone. She had a couple of days off and would be spending them with Declan. This was her only chance to get a few minutes just for herself. She had thought that Amy would still be asleep – what nineteen year-old is up before midday when they're on holiday?

.•. .•. .•.

1.06pm 'Samaritans. Can I help?'

Louise is silent. Her jaw is clamped. She knows the emptiness that is inside. She hurt herself many times as a teenager when her body contained this feeling. The huge abuses enacted on her have led her here before. In the last decade things have been relatively settled but now she is back in crisis once more.

'I'm still here if you want to talk,' says the voice.

'I ... I don't know how to talk right now.'

'Okay, let's not worry about that for a moment, I'm here and I have time to wait.'

'Thanks, it's... ahh ... I'm in real pain here.'

'Are you feeling unwell?'

'No, it's that ... oh my God ... I've ... I've just been attacked.'

'Oh, my dear do you need to go somewhere or is there someone nearby who can help?'

'No! ... No one can ... no one's coming anywhere near me right now – no one. Fuck,' Louise is crying into the phone, 'I'm in such a mess. It happened this morning … still feels like it's just happened.'

The voice on the other end of the phone is soft, gentle, patient.

'It's okay, okay, take your time, there's no hurry here.'

Louise feels some warmth and comfort from the voice on the other end of the line. She has called other organizations in her life but in a real crisis like this it is always to the Samaritans that she turns; they have saved her life many times since she was a teenager.

'Would you like to give me a name I can call you by?'

'Yeah … it's Lou. And your name?'

'If it helps, Jamie.'

'Yes it does Jamie, thanks … thanks for being here.'

'I don't know if you've ever called before but we are always here 24/7, every day of the year, and if you don't feel you can talk, you can email us at jo@samaritans.org.'

Through heaving tears Louise speaks, 'Thanks … yes … I know.'

'Well if it's too much to talk about things at the moment then at least you know how to get hold of us again. But I'm concerned that you need physical help. Can we talk about that?'

'I feel so stupid …'

'What do you feel so stupid about Lou?'

'My daughter told me not to, oh fuck, I don't know what to do right now, I … I … I get it all wrong, I'm such a fucking fool. He wasn't going to lay a finger on me but I stood up, freaked out and then I fucked it all up from there.'

Louise's mind is quickly switching from one past trauma situation to another. She is still in grief for her loss of Marc. She is playing contorted fragments of the night she panicked with him; a benign situation for her has been overlaid and entwined with the malevolent situation she has just endured with Declan.

After almost an hour of making little sense Louise begins to sound angry. She blurts to the Samaritan, 'I've been raped and beaten up by my boyfr … he's nothing to me, he raped me, I just don't know that I want to go through all this again, I'm really thinking about just killing myself.'

'Do you have a plan Louise?'

'Oh, no … no … perhaps that was just a phrase.'

'Louise, this is such a difficult moment in life. If I've understood you, this seems to have been happening to you one way or another all your life. We need to get you safe *now*. Do you know what you might have to do in order to make yourself safe?'

'I want to get in the bath and scrub that fucker out of me; I've been trying to work this out since 9.30 this morning. I'm scratched and torn everywhere. My little girl, she knew he was a bad 'un. I just can't tell the difference it seems. I had a good one and frightened him away, and then I keep this wanker until he does this to me. I only said I didn't want to have sex with him again.' She begins to cry once more, deep, snarling sobs. 'I should … I should be able to fucking decide when and what I want to do with someone. I've got … I've been fucked over like this … my whole life. But then that was the start of it … I thought … I thought I was going … going … going to die.'

For the next thirty minutes Louise recounts the way she was subjected to a torrent of humiliation, forced sexual acts and a beating that has left her bruised from her buttocks to her face. This was her rape, her powerless torture. This was something she never wished to happen to her again. This is not what she wanted from Marc when she asked him to whip her, and this rape bore no relationship with the anal and vaginal acts Marc and her had played out. These were acts of violence and hate against a woman.

Without any specialist training in the trauma of sexual violence, the Samaritan, Jamie, listens and supports Louise through her immediate crisis. She feels safe with the Samaritans and in any event there was no stopping her or suggesting a specialist helpline like Rape Crisis once she had begun.

Jamie's shift is nearing its end.

'Louise, you don't have to go; you can continue talking to us here for as long as you like but my shift is coming to an end in about fifteen minutes. If you want to continue talking that's fine but I will have to pass you over to another listener in that case. It's a woman coming on – Jill – and I could tell her what's been going on for you so that you don't have to repeat yourself; I could do the changeover for you so that you could hear what I was saying to Jill if you want me to.'

Sounding much more calm than at any point in the conversation, Louise says, 'You're very sweet, thank you, but I'll go when you need to go.'

'Okay I respect what you are saying, but I'm still worried about you being alone at the moment; do you know what you want to do about what's happened?'

'I know I should go to the police, stop this bastard, lock him up but …'

'Look, I'm just checking what you can do here on the Internet … The Metropolitan Police have sexual offences specialist trained officers; each borough has dedicated teams to look after women in your situation. They will know so much more than me for instance. From what you've told me it sounds as if you could get Amy to help you? She sounds strong, sorted and capable enough to help her mum right now. Perhaps she could help you get to the station.'

⋅✦⋅ ⋅✦⋅ ⋅✦⋅

5.23pm Louise walks into her bathroom. She undresses looking away from the mirror. It does not take her very long to bruise. Her vagina stings hugely as she sits down on the toilet and urinates – she can hardly bear to wipe herself dry. She is relieved to see that there is no blood on the paper this time. Once she has finished drawing the bath, she pours into the water a few drops of gentle aromatherapy oil that Amy gave her for her birthday and steps in.

19 i want out

'Do you have any idea why you think we keep away from the socio-political conversations, as you call it then?'

'That's what I've been mulling over. It's not like I'm stupid is it? They did teach me something about thinking in all the years I was at university,' Marc laughs. 'I'm interested in the fact that you can always manage to pull back from giving me a personal view about pornography. I treat you like a sponge; I've brought some pretty nasty stuff into this room over the last year – felching, fisting, beatings, ATMs, abuse, suicide, infidelity – and it was all stuck in my head. It was rotting me away; it was closing me off from more and more in my life. But as I drove away from last week's session I thought, what about you? How do you manage all the, pardon my English, *merde* I bring into the room.'

'I'm not certain which question you are asking, Marc. Do you want to explore the socio-political ideas that I agree have been avoided? Are you asking me for my view on pornography? Or are you seeking to know how I deal with difficult material?'

Marc sits with a perplexed expression on his face as if surprised that I have reflected to him three questions – as if he is surprised to learn he has just asked three questions.

'What is it that's so scary here? Haven't I looked under all the stones yet?'

'Scary?'

'It's not about how you deal with the grim stuff; I'm certain your training and therapy did that for you. It's the wider picture and it's what you think about porn that I'm wondering about.'

'These seem like big questions that you want answers to. Let's continue to put what I think about porn to one side. If we work through the *macro* views of pornography I think my own view will probably become irrelevant to you. I don't think it's what you need to know.'

'Maybe that's why I've been scared to get into this stuff; if your view comes out then it might change the space?'

'Are we back to fear of judgement then? Or is there an anxiety about loss?' I ask.

'I believe you in this room; you know how much I have had to trust to this space and therefore to you to go through this process. I'm certain … no … it can't be unusual to …' Marc starts the sentence for the third time '… I can't get away from the idea of how disgusted you, everyone, is, would be, by what I've been into. Even now that I've been "clean" from the Internet for what, seven months, I'm still using hardcore porn, aren't I.'

'Well,' I say, 'if we are to go into the *macro*, to look at the wider view of porn, to take in a view other than yours in this space, it could be a big challenge. I think I'm hearing you say that now you have begun to resensitize yourself you are becoming less comfortable with porn full stop. Not just porn on the Internet but in a more general way.' I pause and then continue, 'Is that right?'

'Back at the start of the year I was so pleased with myself. I had pulled away from Louise – that was difficult, bruising; I didn't want to stop that affair. I thank her for doing it for me. I guess I've come to see her as having looked after me … we've been through this before … But then the big changes started to happen. That day I had the premium rate calls barred on my phone and then when I bought my first mag in a long while, rather than go home and use the net … they all came together with me understanding what was driving me to the Internet and you helping me discover that *I* could stop it for myself.'

'But *now*?' I enquire. When there is no response I continue, 'I've asked you this many times before: What do you want now?'

'I want this process to continue, to go on, to develop, go further … I'm pleased at the marker we crossed by going down to one session a week …' Marc's speech runs out of energy.

'And? But?' I prompt him.

'I need to know what the next bit's all about?'

Silence.

'It seems that it's so much easier for you to be with the extreme than the age-old fear of the unknown. When we talk at the extreme level it somehow focuses you, stops you running away; the extreme seems to stop you fearing the unknown. But now, you're skirting around it all.'

Silence.

What is this about you, Marc? I'm not impatient with you but I do wonder why you still can't take the risk of looking at the big picture of your involvement with pornography. You raise the question and then you retire from it. Time and again it gets raised in tacit ways but even here when you explicitly bring it into the room you run away as quickly as possible. To have given up the telephone sex chat, to have 'lost' Louise, to have stopped using the net for porn, to be engaged with Judy for the first time in years – big steps, well taken, but what can't I see? Why do you struggle with the macro *so much?*

Marc wriggles in the chair, then he coughs, pours some more water into the glass he has been drinking from. 'I don't know … even with things … no … umm …'

Silence.

My body is beginning to tense up; it's reminiscent of the reactions I've had in anticipation of him dropping a 'trauma bomb' in the room.

Silence.

'It's not that this is difficult like when … it's not more "stuff" …' He pushes his fingers through his hair.

Am I judging you as I sit here, Marc? Is this a question for my supervisory space? What would I take? What could I find out that I can't see here? How would I phrase the enquiries?

My supervisory queries might start with judgement, but there is a lot here that seems to be about intimacy of course, and the desensitization – though these are both issues that are moving. You report that we have done some good work over the last year but you bring up the wider-world questions of how pornography fits in society; yes, stuff I'm interested in enough to engage with you about, but then you fail to make the connection with what you label this central issue … Can it be a central issue? You are at the centre, your behaviours. I want to stick with that idea. Yes, the socio-political issues of what pornography does to the user, to the partner and on into other relationships is central somehow …

Epiphany! Right in front my nose.

Despite your intelligence Marc, despite the discipline you have shown and the way you have grown with regard to sympathy for Louise, and even recently the empathy that has been evident with regard to Judy, you have never really let us connect with the issues about that girl in the puffa jacket; you have never really admitted the deeper issue that so affected you by witnessing that particular piece of extreme pornography because to do so might mean you would have to walk away from all pornography; you have remained involved in its use because you have tuned out from the fact that this stuff is produced by using people at least as badly abused as …

Marc shifts in his chair, as if aware of my internal dialogue.

Silence.

… Louise and yourself. The women you have watched on the Internet, that you watch in your DVD collection and that you masturbate to in your new hardcore porn magazines are the Louises of the world. That's a very tearful feeling. You need to find this Marc … you need to make this connection. Perhaps I can help you get to this point today; perhaps you need a nudge from me to start you off.

Silence.

'I want out of looking at porn totally,' Marc finally says. 'That turned out to be very difficult to say. I think I really do need out. I can't just do a little bit of porn – it's not what I'm doing all of this work for – but I don't know how to stop completely. I'm pleased with where I find myself in comparison to last year, but I don't know how to move forward to the next level because,' Marc coughs, 'it's like porn's okay here. Does that make any sense? It seems like you not giving me your view of what you think of porn holds me back.'

'Marc, *you* are okay here, you can bring what you need to, you can say whatever you need to say, but I've never suggested in this space that hardcore or extreme pornography is okay. I know what it is and understand it from my work but I've never said it was okay.'

I glance at the clock; there are thirty minutes remaining before the session ends – enough time to begin to discuss the *macro* world of the effects, the traumas and the devastations that the porn industry can create for susceptible users, to say nothing of the men and women who perform in it and the ripples it pushes out into the mainstream of society.

'It seems that you *want* me, that you *need* me, to prime this next part of your recovery,' I say. 'I think you know what the porn industry – softcore, hardcore and extreme – can do to people. I think you know because you have experienced the effects of it as a user over many years. It's not my place to take up an "anti" position. Indeed, I'm even certain that there are better ways to challenge and seek change over an exploitative industry than censorship or outright bans.

'Let me ask you a question, Marc. When you sit down in your office chair at the start of the day what's your risk of dying as a result?'

'Interesting question. I like it when you bowl me a spinner. I like it when I don't know where a question leads. I could answer it from several positions but I think they'd be flippant responses. Short of something freak happening, my chances are no more, and possibly less, than in the rest of my day-to-day life – certainly less than on my drive to work down the A14.'

'Exactly. Yet when people in the sex industry turn up for work, when porn actors and actresses walk in front of the camera, they put themselves at risk. I think I'm correct in quoting to you that on average almost 90 per cent of US porn is produced without performers using a condom. That constantly puts those performers one sexual encounter away from the risk of contracting chlamydia, hepatitis C, syphilis, gonorrhoea, HIV. And that's to say nothing of the risks to women or gay men who perform ATMs, or the possible physical injury that occurs through overly rough and double or multiple anal penetrations and fistings.'

'I guess I know the arguments; they're well rehearsed, aren't they?' Marc says.

'"These are consensual acts"; "People go into it for the money" and so on *ad nauseam*. Are those the ones you have in mind?'

'I've used them on myself. Somehow, most of all I still find it difficult to get away from the idea that getting paid for it makes it okay.'

'Well, pause for a moment, Marc. Imagine if you had not had opportunities in your life, if you had had no good fortune – how different might your life have been? Imagine how differently you might have expressed the anger you had in you, if you'd not had the opportunity to verbalize your thoughts and feelings. What might you have done? How might your life have been different?'

Silence.

Marc nods as if running the scenarios through in his head.

'I guess I can see you heading towards Louise with this; her opportunities have been pretty slim.'

'Yes … while she is naturally a smart woman, the opportunities she's been given in life have been very limited. She's always been vulnerable in so many ways, not least of which she had children to support. Although someone will always argue that there are women seemingly in her position who don't turn to sex work to make a living, to me her abusive past made her vulnerable – like cannon fodder for some part of the industry.'

'People abused in childhood have had their boundaries violated?'

'Yes, sometimes they can recover from that – perhaps you might consider yourself doing that in this process – but others have had their boundaries smashed, crushed and destroyed. By rule of thumb, the more damage that remains, obviously the more vulnerable a person is.'

I lean forward and slide open a drawer in the oak coffee table in front of me and take out some printed pages of quotes compiled from the Internet. I read some extracts to Marc. Almost invariably the porn actresses and the prostitutes describe how, as children, they were abused. These are stories of psychological, physical and/or sexual degradation. The paragraphs tell how uncles fingered their nieces, how brothers raped sisters and how fathers and mothers beat daughters until they ran away from home – exposed, unsophisticated young women are open to exploitation at the hands of people who claim they will help them out.

I give Marc a passage to read to himself. It is about a fifteen year-old female prostitute who was systematically raped by a gang of pae-dophiles. 'It's virtually Louise isn't it?' he says to me.

For a few minutes we exchange, mainly aloud, vignettes that come from porn actresses who report the degradation of their occupation and how it made them feel. There is tangible anger from Marc as he reads the case against a man who committed a violent rape but was acquitted because his victim had worked both as a prostitute and in the sex industry. 'Fuck, it's like she's got no human rights left. That makes me feel fucking mad.'

Marc is so able to identify with the victim element of these stories – the self within. But as his use of extreme and hardcore pornography shows it is also easy for him to get turned on and tune out to the suf-fering of victims of pornography. Today's session is a head-on assault on this position.

'These are not statements from radical feminists blaming men for the ills of the world. These are the painful words written by damaged women. They hurt me to read and perhaps they should hurt any indi-vidual who claims to be part of this society. I think there is even a case to be made that we *all* have a responsibility to change things – men and women.'

'Aahh, I should be much more aware of this! I should know that these things happen.'

'And we should seek ways to protect people from the underlying causes. The damage done to people like you and Louise, the abusive sections of your lives, are perhaps what have made you both particu-larly susceptible to getting lost in the pornized world.'

I consider balancing the view I have just given Marc with some reports of the damage men have also suffered in the world of pornog-raphy and prostitution, but time in the session is running short and I want to share with Marc one more passage chosen as it might help him to link to the confusion and pain he felt when he watched the film of the Eastern European girl in the puffa jacket. It's by Svea Nova, an ex-porn star active in the German and international porn film market from 2000 to 2006. She appeared in numerous extreme hardcore and fetish films and ten BDSM films, the best known of which is *Dungeon disgrace – the suffering of Svea Nova*. I read out loud an extract from the introduction to her autobiography *Suffering for life*.

> I've taken part in many extreme shoots. Perhaps you've seen me in one of them; I'm the one taking the double or even triple penetration. Perhaps you saw me when I got slapped in the face, full force, or one of the ones where the guy spits in my face or spits in my pussy. You don't remember me? How about all the movies where I get called a bitch and I tell you, the viewer, that I love it when I get degraded like this, that I love it so much and that I deserve the 'punishment' because I'm a stupid, dirty, worthless slut, a whore, a bitch in heat. Still you don't remember me? I've been fisted and fucked at the same time; I've had two cocks in my arse. I drank urine until it made me vomit while a group of 'studs' laughed at me. Still don't remember me? Oh well, no one looks after you in that profession and no one cares who you are. If they choke you with their cocks, if they hurt you as they ram into your holes or rick your neck as they pile drive you, no one cares, as long as you can hold the position they want you to. As long as you keep smiling at the camera and saying how much you like all the things they are doing to you or as long as you keep wincing in pain, crying as they film your degradation, you know it's okay – smiling makes it all consensual; it lets them degrade you more. Cringing, wincing, crying makes you into the actress. When they stop hurting you, at the end of the movie, you turn to the camera and say how much you enjoy it: it stops it being rape; it stops it being abuse; it makes you an actress, not a prostitute.
>
> I used to think to myself, as long as I can walk away from this at the end of the day, as long as they pay me, I'm alright, I'm looking after myself aren't I? Look how grown up I am; I'm an actress and one day I'll be in other types of films and one day I'll be a film-maker. One day I'll be important if I just keep doing this.
>
> But those girls from further east … seeing them – how they got used in the industry – helped me get out. Can you think what it's like to be in a German film when you hardly speak a word of German? You only speak your own language. Nothing else makes sense. Everyone is pushing you to do this, waving a few extra euros in your face – if you will just do this.

Those poor girls didn't even know what they were agreeing to. That was the last straw for me. These kids had no experience, they had no idea. NO idea. You could tell they'd never even been in a film before. And here they were, thrown in at the deep end. They were getting a DP, getting a fist up their ass. I even saw one girl getting double fisted in the first scene she'd ever shot – fucking barbaric. At the end she was frightened, terrified, and bleeding.

[…]

Anyway, I had had enough of it. I'd seen one too many girls from Eastern Europe crying, crying with the shock and trauma. I could suddenly see myself four or five years before. It made me sick to see what I was doing to myself. I got cleaned up, got away from the drink and the drugs. I found myself real help and support, and now I'm back getting an education, now I'm doing some proper study so I can do something with my life. I started to write it out of me, and this is my story of recovery.

'Powerful stuff isn't it?'

'I'm humbled but I'm glad you read that to me.'

'Thankfully there is a growing amount of material to read and view online like this Marc.' I slide across the tabletop a slip of paper on which I've listed some useful sites he can read or watch. 'These sites all have accounts from former porn actors and actresses who have moved away from the business. 'If you go looking for yourself you'll find there are a lot of right-wing Christians sites you might want to avoid. I say that mainly because their message is to censor and ban pornography. If this were to happen it would be sent underground and I hate to think what that would ultimately encourage to happen if it were the case.

'Actually, I also don't know if you are up to the radical feminist sites yet – even though I think there is a lot you might learn from the radical camp.'

·•· ·•· ·•·

Working with men like Marc teaches me that it's pointless to blame men for the difficulties women suffer. He began life (as we have often said in my consulting room) as the victim of a woman. I want to make clear that I am not an apologist for misogynists. I am an *equalitist*, and life in the adult world of therapy tells me that thoughtful people would like to see equality for both sexes, for their sons as well as for their daughters. There are many men we could blame for the degradation of women, but if you alienate men – the group of society that I would suggest most needs to be engaged with, educated, and encouraged to develop and change their views – you are likely to perpetuate the situation we currently find our society in. (This knowledge complicates what some women want to make out is a simple picture; these are misandrists who certainly hold a lot of sway in the 'anti' porn camp.)

Experience and practice shows me that it is far easier to 'set' a human being in his or her ways than it is to change them. The view that 'men are the problem' dilutes the reality that society is made up of men and women, and that there are millions of powerless men and women in our society. Surely we should be working towards an end of degradation wherever, whenever and to whomever it happens. If we blame only men for pornography, we fail to engage with the complexity of the argument and we fail to take responsibility for the pornized society we have all allowed or even encouraged to come into existence.

•◆• •◆• •◆•

'The radical camp,' I say to Marc, 'might still be a confusing place to visit as yet but the first site on the list is the best if you want to engage with some feminist thought.' For a moment, in my head I find it bizarre that I might be protecting Marc from the full force of a radical feminist site when, for so many years, he has been able to stomach hardcore and extreme porn.

'There are many kinds of smoke screens put up by people to persuade you this is this and that is that,' I say. There are women who support porn and say it's sexual empowerment, misogynists who claim these girls do it because they like it, porn actresses who make documentaries about how awful the business is but then retract their story because they stay in the industry, and many points in between. But whenever you get lost in the field, so as to speak, go to the final link on the list and you can read Svea's account again to keep you on track.'

'Why is it so hard for a man like me to find the truth about porn but so easy to find the most bizarre and unusual kinds of the stuff? Ask me to find that picture of a woman with "a fill in the blank" inserted in her "fill in the blank" and I can do it. If you'd ever have asked me to go and find these pages of quotes …'

'And now you have to decide where you want to draw the line on what is pornography and what isn't, or perhaps you will be happy to separate out erotica from pornography if you think that's possible. Now you really have to think whether you want to give up using pornography or give up looking at any image of a woman that might make you want to masturbate to it. You will have to decide whether such images make women into objects or whether there are exceptions. As you continue to resensitize yourself, the possibilities will continue to open up in front of you and we can talk about all of them.'

Silence.

'Better sign me up for another year then – June 2009 here we come!' Marc smiles. I smile back.

Silence.

For a moment before we end the session Marc sits with his eyes gently closed, breathing deeply, his fingertips set in a triangle, thumb to thumb, tip to tip. We both know there are struggles ahead, but for the moment there is peace in the room.

4 July 2009

9.38am The gravel crackles under Louise's feet as she walks back through the hotel garden to her room in a separate block from the main hotel. She unlocks the door. The fruit compote is gurgling in her guts as it mixes with the freshly squeezed orange juice and the white and brown toast she had spread with thick cut marmalade and rich yellow butter. It is the same breakfast menu she ate the morning after she ejected Marc from her life. And now she enters the same bedroom in which they last had sex. The full-length windows look onto the hotel garden; it is greener than when he lay beside her. The trees are now rich in their summer hues. The view registers somewhere inside of Louise but she is not really sitting on the bed today; she is not really anywhere right now.

•◆• •◆• •◆•

It's the first time in many years that things could really be thought of as 'in order' for Louise.

She was pleased she had accepted Marc's money for Amy the last time they met all those months ago. She is aware that the money could have been seen as blackmail; she is aware that it could have burned into her, forming a prostitute. However, she holds herself back from that personal ignominy by believing that Marc did in fact love her and that he wanted to help what she loved – her beautiful daughter, about whom he had heard so much, with whom he had engaged by suggesting so many helpful things.

Although there was a short period when Louise had wanted to destroy Marc, she knew in reality they could not be together. Although she didn't want to take his money, she knew where the relationship was heading. She knew that therapy was making Marc consider his actions. And she knew there was rightness to his shift away from her. She had always been honest when she said to Marc that she didn't want to cause a split between him and Judy. For a time she had hoped she might get to share him, and she had certainly let herself fantasize that Judy would leave Marc and then he would want Louise to be with him. She even fantasized there might be a way in which the three of them could be involved together in a relationship.

Despite the care Louise had often felt Marc showed towards her, if she had been asked how she really felt about men she was aware that, in a sexual sense at least, they did still revolt her. As she has grown older she has become more aware that satisfaction might be found between the legs of a woman rather than another man. The excitement for her is in the softness of a woman's body, the 'perfumed' essence, the gentleness of the frame.

When Louise had seen the photograph of Judy and Marc during her stay at their Norfolk home, she felt a relationship with Judy would have been possible. For months after that difficult weekend Louise fantasized about speaking to Judy on the telephone and then forming a pact with her in which they would entice Marc into their web, where they would entrap him, bind him, rape him and then perform a male vision of lesbian love in front of his enfeebled body. The two of them would ravish each other's body until he was forced to become erect and then Judy would take her revenge on his penis in the manner she felt most appropriate. But all of these things had faded in Louise's mind over recent months. As the time passed she knew with increasing certainty that there would be no other outcome than the one that had already unfolded; she knew that she could never have had Marc, even less both of them.

⁘ ⁘ ⁘

When Louise left the house yesterday morning she gave Amy £100 cash and told her not to worry if she didn't return until Sunday evening. Over the last few weeks Louise had been putting her affairs in order and she had subtly told Amy where everything was kept – all the financial information Amy might need and, in particular, she showed her where there was an account with the money that would effectively allow her to take up the place she wanted at Oxford. Later that day, Louise slipped a note in the passbook wallet.

Amy kissed her mother. 'I really love you mum,' she said.

'That's just the £100 speaking my darling little girl,' Louise replied.

'Where you going?'

'I'm going up to Norfolk.'

'You're not getting back with Marc are you? He's a bastard dangling stuff in front of you then vanishing. He hurt you mum.'

Louise leans forward towards Amy; she kisses her on the centre of the forehead. 'You don't need to know some things about my life, sweetie, but I think he really loved me, just wouldn't have been right to take him away from his wife.'

'He didn't get a prize from me!'

Louise's eyes are filled with tears; she kisses her little girl again. 'How did you get to be so grown up? Nineteen years old and yet it seems like only yesterday I was wrapping you up for your first day at school – soon you'll be at university.'

'I'll be back to see you every weekend mum – don't you worry.'

'You won't have to bother with all that,' Louise says turning away.

Louise had not really wanted to talk to Amy this morning, not this morning of all mornings. She had planned that Amy would still be asleep – what nineteen year-old is up before midday unless they have to be?

•◆• •◆• •◆•

9.40am 'Samaritans. Can I help?'

Louise is silent. Her jaw is clamped. She knows the emptiness that is inside. She hurt herself many times as a teenager when her body contained this feeling. The huge disappointments she has always felt used to lead her here. In the last decade things have settled but she is in the middle of a plan much greater now. This is the same as the feeling that drove her to Beachy Head, but that day she had met a lovely woman who made her feel safe, made her feel that there was someone who cared for her, even if it was just for a few moments. This time Louise is determined not to see or speak to anyone. But she does want to tell someone what she is about to do before she arrives at her final destination. She is not certain why, but she wants to talk. Perhaps there will be the right voice, a voice that will understand what she is going to do.

'I'm still here if you want to talk,' says the voice.

'Yes, I know, thank you.'

'How are things?'

'You know, *comme ci, comme ça*.' It is one of Marc's phrases.

'If you'd like to talk about it I'm here to listen.'

Louise feels the voice is doing well. It didn't say, 'I'm *happy* to listen to you.' She hates it when she hears disingenuous phrases like that. *Who could be happy to listen about my life?*

'Thanks, that would be good. Life's a strange place right now; everything that needs paying up *is* paid up. There's a few quid in the building society for my daughter. She's a smart cookie; she knows where she's going. My son's got a good job. Wish I could have ever said that for myself.'

The voice gives out warming affirmations that it's listening to her.

'He's doing a management development programme; I'm very proud of him.'

There is a long silence. After a while the voice says to Louise, 'I'm still here.'

'Yes, I know,' she replies, 'me too, I work on telephone lines as well.'

'Oh, I see, so you know how it is – speaking to strangers.'

'Sort of … I'm a telephone tart you know. I offer men, sometimes women, a voice to masturbate to.'

Without any pause the voice says, 'I imagine that might be difficult.'

In a matter-of-fact tone Louise replies, 'It doesn't matter, I'm off to kill myself in a few minutes.'

'So you are feeling very suicidal at the moment, is that right?'

'I'm going to kill myself in about half an hour. I don't want you to stop me. I've thought about it, I just want to tell someone. I'm sat down on my bed here in the hotel, everything is neatly packed up so they can send it back home, I don't have to go very far to do it.'

'So you have a plan of how you are going to kill yourself?'

'Oh yes, I'm going over the cliff properly this time. It's funny I had planned to lay here on my bed and masturbate to the gorgeous thoughts I have about the last man to break my heart but I didn't feel like it once I'd laid down. It seemed stupid somehow to engage with sex this close to the end. It's the thing that's brought me all the worst things in my life.'

'Do you think we could talk about those worst things? I'm very concerned to hear that you think there are no options in life.'

'Look, I can put the phone down if you are going to ask me all these questions. You don't have a clue what cliff I'm going to jump off; it could be into the Avon Gorge, it could be Beachy Head, you don't have a clue. I don't want to be rude, but this is the last conversation I'm ever going to have. I know it's tough on you but I just want to say what I'm going to do, then I'm going to do it. I doubt that it will make the headlines anywhere. I'm just a faceless old bird who killed herself at a time when to the outside world it looked like things were quite neat and tidy.'

'Do you mind if I know your name?' says the voice.

'So that you can make more of a connection with me? Well, if you like. Loulou's my name. But give up trying to stop me. I want you to know what I'm going to do that's all – what's your name?'

'Alex,' the voice replies quickly.

'Look I have written a note to my ex-lover; he'll never get it. I've written one to my son and one to my daughter. I'm just pinning them to the left side of my chest, over my heart. Alex, don't ask a question please. I'm wearing a black satin blouse that my lover liked seeing me in; I was wearing it the first time I saw him and the first time we had sex. Now I'm going to die in it.'

Alex is clearly overtaken with the emotion that is present in the call. Louise can hear it in Alex's breath pattern. Louise has listened to so many people breathe it told her how far from orgasm they were. She feels she could tell a life story just from listening to breath.

'Please, think about it Loulou. Why not stay and talk to me, see if you might want to … want to change your mind.'

'I've got my MP3 set to repeat our favourite track. I've got the notes pinned to me. My make-up is just about perfect. And even if I say so myself, I think I look pretty good.'

'What's your daughter's name, Loulou?'

'Oh come on Alex, it's a trick. I'm going to go now.'

'Loulou, you can stay. I just thought you might want to tell me the name of the important people in your life?'

'My daughter – she could be a model but thank God she has a brain. Her name's Amy. My son is David, I love him very much as well. Never really had a good man in my life until I met Marc. I know it sounds pathetic, like some really bad soap. No, I'm not killing myself because of Marc; more that he was the last chance I'd given myself. Everyone's let me down. My life has been a fucking mess from the start, abused as a child, as an adult. Two lovely children I've had but my son is involved in his own life and my girl will be somewhere else before the end of the year. Everyone leaves me. Marc wasn't even mine to have, just a gorgeous man who ended up showing me that I've had more than enough of life. Since we are always on our own no matter what we do, I've taken my girl as far as she really needs me. So it's time to fuck off out of this life now. I'm not killing myself because of Marc … more because of what he pointed out. I had to tell him to go, that I didn't want him, but the truth is I wanted him too much. He could only have failed me so I let him go so that at least Judy and him could have a good life.'

'Who is Judy? Is that Marc's wife?'

Louise cuts the call. 'Thank you Alex,' she says into the dead mobile handset.

Louise changes her underwear. Ever since she was a child, ever since she can remember dressing herself, any emotive situation has led her to change her pants as soon as possible as if removing the trauma in her undergarment. As a teenager she wore two pairs at once so she always had a spare pair wherever she was. A visit to the toilet would allow her to take off both pairs then put the pair that had been on the outside back on. Once Louise had some money of her own coming in, when she was a teenager, she would buy economy packs of knickers so she could discard what she felt were the soiled pair each time she needed to. She also thought that somehow wearing more than one pair at once might protect her. Today she had put on some silk ones – after all, she thought, *someone's going to find me, may as well try and look nice down there one final time. If I'm laid out there on the beach I'd like to look nice in the place where all the trouble in life's come from.*

•➤• •➤• •➤•

10.23am Louise steps over the first line of green wire fencing to the cliff edge not far from the lighthouse café. She sees the sign for the Samaritans. 'SAMARITANS Telephone 08457 909090 Visit or write: King's Lynn …' She blows Alex a kiss; they will not help her now. A blue hot hatch rolls into the car park as Louise crosses the second fence. The couple in the vehicle give a concerned look in her direction as they get out. The man shouts something at Louise but she does not hear him. Her MP3 is on full volume as she moves more swiftly over the second wire fence. The man begins to run towards her but no one is going to save her this time. She is at the cliff edge before he has reached the first fence. The music playing in her ears cuts out the sound of the sea birds nesting in the cliff face. She looks up into the clear blue sky, before looking down. The sun has not yet dried the surface of the sand. She half expects a hand on her shoulder as she steps forward.

21 here again

4 July 2009

9.38am Sunlight struggles to make its way through the heavy curtains in Louise's bedroom. The alarm snooze cycle clicks in one more time as she covers her head with the white cotton-covered pillow. *Fuck, Friday and I've got to work.* Louise hates covering for other girls on the telephone line. *At least it's not for the first shift of the day. Two more minutes and I'll get up.* The landing floorboards creak as Amy and her boyfriend begin the descent of the staircase. Louise hears the front door close – Henry has left. As she lies in bed she can hear Amy is in the kitchen. Her sweet teenage voice sings out a ten year-old pop tune. *She's so unlike me. How did I ever get such a happy, sorted girl?* Louise drifts in and out of consciousness. Somewhere in her mind she is thinking of Amy as a toddler. Her mind registers that she's dreaming – not really with her sweet little girl, not really anywhere right now.

•◦• •◦• •◦•

It's the first time in a long while that Louise has found herself thinking about Marc. A punter who has taken to phoning her during her afternoon shifts somehow reminds her of him. The caller is inventive, gentle and seems genuinely interested in her. It feels like he knows how to play the same game as Marc did.

In an idle moment Louise stops to think how many men out there might behave like Marc. It annoys her that some of them can get through her defences so easily; Owen will become one of them. If Louise thought about it further, she would realize that it's probably because it makes her feel like a real human being, and whenever it happens she is aware that she judges herself; it forces her to look at why she is selling her sexual desires and proclivities; it makes her feel like a prostitute. *There is nothing wrong with being a prostitute* Louise reasons with herself, *the oldest profession* ... But when she sees herself in this light it makes her realize the control others have over her when she has put herself in this position.

Over the past eighteen months or so, since she last met Marc, the money she extracted from him has weighed heavily on her. From the moment she forced the payment from him in her final post on the Island she had intended it to be for Amy – the money that would help her through university – but finances were really tight a year and a half ago. The day after she arrived back from Norfolk, she considered putting the money into a bond, locking it up so that it was separated out for Amy.

Life has a way of dealing Louise blows and four days later the washing machine needed fixing; the 'ashtray (almost) on wheels' needed some welding done, two new tyres and an exhaust system if it was going to get through its MOT; and perhaps most important her current account needed to be brought out of the serious overdraft situation it was in. Little by little the things added up.

How much would you really blackmail a man like Marc for? Eight thousand pounds is loose change to him. If you spend £70,000 on a car that you call a toy, how much should you spend on your mistress? How much could you spend on prostitutes?

∙◆∙ ∙◆∙ ∙◆∙

The guilt about spending Amy's money rises to the front of Louise's mind sometimes. Yesterday morning she gave Amy £100 cash and told her to go and enjoy spending it on something to look good in. Over the last few months Louise has been putting her affairs in order and from different sources she has managed to build Amy a small fund of almost £2,000. Louise sat and talked to her daughter about how she wanted to help her with everything she can. She has shown her the building society passbook with the money she has put to one side for her. However, Amy was ahead of her mother. She applied, and was accepted, for a well-paid post for someone of her age and experience before she even told Louise about getting a job. Despite what Louise might think, Amy is fully aware of the inconsistency with which her mother's money is earned and she is building herself the biggest cash reserve she can before she begins at Oxford. Amy is even prepared to defer her place if she needs to in order to put herself in the best possible position.

Amy kisses her mother. 'I really love you mum,' she says.

'That's just the £100 speaking,' Louise replies.

'No I just love my mum and I'm not going to be around here much longer so I want you to know that. I'm putting that £100 in the account. I can do without new clothes right now.'

Louise leans forward towards Amy; she kisses her on the centre of the forehead. 'It's nice to know someone loves me, honey.'

'You get all the prizes from me!'

Louise's eyes are filled with tears; she kisses her little girl again. 'How did you get to be so grown up? Nineteen years old and yet it seems like only yesterday I was wrapping you up for your first day at school – soon you'll be at university.'

'I'll be back to see you every weekend mum – don't you worry.'

'You won't have to bother with all that,' Louise says turning away from Amy.

Louise has been pleased to talk to Amy this morning. Amy is normally asleep when Louise has breakfast or she has already left home for work. Louise just wishes that Amy could be on holiday like her friends right now. What nineteen year-old wants to be up before midday?

I should have squeezed Marc for every penny.

·•· ·•· ·•·

1.00pm 'Hello.'

'Hiya.'

'Hi darling; are you alright?'

'I'm not too bad thank you.'

'God, you sound lovely, so who am I speaking to?'

'My name's Owen.'

'My name's Loulou, Owen.'

'Hi Owen umm… I … I mean Loulou,' the rather gentle voice laughs at his mistake.

'Hi Owen.'

Owen's mistake makes Louise feel warm towards her caller: 'Ahh, you sound really nice.' Her tone is motherly, affectionate.

'What do you look like?'

'Well, do you like a lady with some curves?' she asks.

'I actually love a lady with some real curves. Ummmh.'

'Right, well, I'm a petite lady, but with the right curves. I'm just a little 'un, about five foot two,' she says, 'but you can always stick a pair of high heels on me if you don't want to bend down to catch my beautiful red lips. I'm brunette, I've got big green eyes and I'm a very curvy, 32C, 28, 38 – that's petite but with real woman's hips,' she says, giving her much used Mae West tone.

'Ohh, I'd like to be looking straight at that beautiful figure, I'd be stiff in a second.'

'Good, I'm glad, now tell me what else you'd like Owen, come on … don't be a shy little boy!'

'Ohhhhhh, I like … I like to go out with girls pubbing, clubbing ummmmm …'

There is something about the gentleness in Owen's voice that allows Louise to imagine him as an eighteen year-old innocent. In her instant rolling fantasy she imagines them not letting him past the step if he turned up to a pub, let alone a club. She begins to run a story in her mind of him being fearful of beginning his sexual encounters with women. His gentleness, almost timidity, becomes attractive. She imagines him to look like a teenage version of Marc.

Louise interrupts Owen.

'Where are you calling from?'

'Me, umm, I'm in Reading.'

'Are you now? I'm in London so we aren't that far apart,' she teases him. 'How old are you honey?'

'Me, I'm uhh, twenty-five.'

'*Are* you?' she teases again.

'Yes, how old are you?'

'I'm quite a bit older than you. You do like your women to be older than you don't you Owen?'

'Ohhhh yeah …'

'Good. Go on then, have a guess how old I am?'

'Ohh, thirty-five?' Owen replies.

'I'm actually older than that my dear.'

'No.'

'Yes I am,' Louise replies in a peek-a-boo style. 'I'm forty-three.'

Louise is beginning to find her role in this – a busty aunt. It suits her mood well. She likes the idea of breaking in a young man and is playing him into his role, too. But she is aware of a particular feeling – a feeling all too familiar to her. It is the feeling she had when she first spoke to Marc, something about connecting her own desire with that of the caller. She is ready to play out a version of Owen's MILF fantasy.

'Forty-three, wow.'

In that reply it is as if, just for a moment, Louise gets a glimpse of an excellent player of sexual games. As if the teenager is really a smart middle-aged man disguising himself in order to play with her. Almost immediately she abandons herself to the game.

'So, you know I'm a curvy lady; what does Owen look like?'

'I'm about six foot one; I've got short dark hair, blue eyes, I'm just under fourteen stone and I've got a satisfyingly thick cock for you Loulou.'

'So what would you like to do with me if I was in the bedroom with you right now? What would you like to do with that satisfyingly thick *cock*?'

'Well you sound like you've got a nice round spankable bum to me.'

'Oooooh, did you hear my intro?'

'No,' Owen lied.

'Well that's a pity 'cos I mention how much I like a good firm spanking …'

'Really?'

'Oh yes, I like to be spanked sometimes.'

'Oooh, I like that Loulou.'

'It's feeling very round and spankable right now – do you know why?'

'No. Why?'

'Because my beautiful tight silk panties are encasing my soft warm flesh.'

'Ooooh God! What colour are they?'

'Have a guess …' Louise is beginning to record some detail about Owen. Two minutes forty seconds into the call and she can already tell how hooked he is; his breathing pattern tells her how erect his penis is becoming and she knows she is getting inside his head – a long call with lots of miniature climaxes on the way to the final big one is what she has planned for him. At the end of the call he will be hooked, of that she is certain.

'Have a guess …'

'Ummm, black?'

Louise replies instantly with a huge intake of breath, 'Yes! How did you know!'

'Ummmhhh, can you … could you bend over in them for me?'

'Well you know what happens when I bend over in these silk knickers?'

'Oooohhhh.'

'My bum cheeks just push to the edge of the material; it encases my tight, tight cheeks.'

'Ohhhh God, yes, yes can you just give those cheeks a slap for me?'

'You'd like me to spank myself for you, Owen?'

'God, yes, yes please.'

'How many times would you like me to smack that naughty bottom for you?'

'Three times, Loulou, three times.'

'And shall I count them out for you.'

'Oh dear god, yes count them out for me.'

'Let me put you on speakerphone so I can move about more, my love. Now you have to promise not to get too excited, Owen, there is a lot more to come before a naughty little boy like you is allowed to shoot the cream from his hot little weapon.'

For the first time in many months Louise is on top of her game. She feels so very alive at this moment. If Owen were to ejaculate too quickly it would be a disaster for her own pleasure. She reaches across to the bookshelf on her left and switches on the minidisc recorder – this is a conversation she thinks she might want to keep.

There is a sharp percussive sound 'one', again a slapping sound 'two', a final smack, 'three, owww'.

Nine times out of ten, Louise would simply clap her hands, act the protest vocally, but despite herself she is already excited at some level by this conversation and so she has bent herself over her own office chair, pulled her skirt up and landed the heaviest blow she can on her own buttocks. Years of experimentation inform her that it is extremely difficult to spank, cane or whip her own arse with the necessary force to achieve the desired relief that is brought when someone else does it to you. However, Louise has made a passable sound for Owen and there is a comforting sting in her cheeks for herself.

'Is that sore?' Owen asks.

'Ooohh it's stinging now, you'll have to rub it better for me.'

'Let me kiss it better as well.'

'Oh I'd love it if you kissed it better. My poor bottom needs some kissing better …'

•◆• •◆• •◆•

7.23pm Louise pours herself a large vodka with a dash of tonic. She drops in an ice cube, returns to her chair and flicks her logbook open. The total time spent on the phone has been good – bonuses for her conversations with Paul, Jake and Owen but after the excitement she felt while working with Owen she now feels alone and lonely. She checks her mobile phone; there are no texts. She flicks her Internet browser open and checks her emails. There are six messages – all of them spam. She clicks her music folder. The application opens and she navigates down the playlists where she hovers over 'The Don' for a moment. She clicks on the second track. It's a recording of their third call together. It's one of her favourites because it's the one where they imagine having sex in the four-poster bed. David had shown Louise how she could use one of her computer programs to import a spoken track and put music underneath it. Track 2 has Marc and Louise's favourite music as an underscore to their aural lovemaking.

You know girl, I really should dump this stuff if I don't want to find myself starting with all this shit again. I need a real fucking life. Perhaps I should give therapy another go. I really do have to find a way forward. Come on! Find a way to take just one small step forward.

epilogue

'When did pornography begin?' asked a reader.
'Long before Marc and Louise were born,' came my answer.
'When will pornography end?' the reader asked.
'With the end of humankind,' came my reply.

Turned On has simply been a map that charts the journey of two souls (Marc and Louise) affected by abuse, trauma, pornography and the search for love. You have stood witness to intimate parts of both of their lives. When you left Marc, in the middle of 2008, he was clearly changing his life. It is for you to decide whether it will become a change for the better. What I do know is, he was becoming a sensitive person in an increasingly desensitized society.

Perhaps Marc's desensitization had begun the day Gareth passed him those hardcore pornographic images in the playground of his junior school. Or perhaps, as a susceptible child, he had already been taken towards the sexualized image through the advertising he saw in glossy women's magazines – images of women produced to sell products to women.

In 1965, the year before Marc was born, 'Mary Quant gives you the bare essentials' showed a naked seated woman – one leg in front of the nipple of her left breast, the other crossed on the floor, her whole body covered in stylized daisies. It was an image using the female form to advertise make-up. Like thousands of other adverts have, and still do, it sold a product that is (almost) exclusively for women, to women, by sexualizing the female form. The advert, with its deep shadow, suggests a voyeurism of the model's body, and it was just such material that fuelled Marc towards his early pornographic searches. In another sort of family, 'the page 3 lovelies' might have formed the same sort of template for him.

Of course, sexual interest is natural and, for centuries, artistic images have also served to portray the male and female form in erotic and sexualized images. As a child, Marc visited art galleries and his father's books also primed his sexual interests. Lovis Corinth's *Friends* (1904) and Paul Delvaux's *Two Girls* (1946) modelled lesbian fantasies for him. Allen Jones' *Girl Table* (1969), which shows a mannequin of a short-haired woman on her hands and knees ('doggie' position) in long black gloves, black boots, and black and yellow corset looking into a mirror on the floor with a plate glass table top on her back, and Sebastiano Del Piombo's *Martyrdom of St Agatha* (1520), which depicts the saint's nipples being tortured with metal pincers, fuelled his interest in fetishistic images. Although a few people might categorize all or some of these images as sexual, erotic or lascivious (even pornographic) long before the invention of the Internet, they are also creative, original and imaginative works of art produced to be looked at by people in the physical presence of the artefact. The Internet – the great delivery tool of twenty-first-century society – has managed to unbalance the 'sweet shop' by transmitting anything available to it to anyone who asks for it.

From the beginning of Marc's work in therapy the course of his life turned towards recovery. While you are witness to just a brief insight to the work he did to resensitize himself, his major stages in recovery are nonetheless recorded here: to take control of himself; to first limit his use of pornography; and then, through many intricate stages, 'retrace' his steps in the pornographic realm. Each reverse step led to reawakening past patterns; each one, eventually, when he was sensitive enough, re-released the excitement it once held and, over time, allowed him to feel turned off by the more extreme materials, seeing them at last for the violence, humiliation and degradation they really are.

As a human being, Louise's story is deeply upsetting. We see the wide sweeping view of someone with a deeply damaged personal social history. As we leave her in July 2009 we have experienced three possible versions of just one day in her life.

The first is the wretched continuation of the pattern of abuse she has experienced throughout life. The therapy space has already met too many Louises shortly after such days.

There is an inevitability to the second version of 4 July 2009. With a borderline personality disorder, Louise has a significantly increased likelihood over the general population of committing suicide. Her experiences and her occupation (where she is isolated as a home worker) effectively allowed her to be continually re-traumatized and abused on an hour-by-hour basis. These simply intensify the risk factors to her.

The final version of that day leaves Louise no further forward than when we first met her. Indeed, it is quite likely that Owen will become her next Marc. Through low levels of formal education, abuse, mental health issues that have not been addressed and relative poverty, Louise remains exposed. There is no neat conclusion to her story.

Marc is set for recovery. Louise appears set to endure the same or even worsening conditions and circumstances – perhaps for the rest of her life – but her last thought *'Find a way to take just one small step forward'* might still give us hope for her.

'When did pornography begin?' asked a reader.
'Long before Marc and Louise were born,' came my answer.
'When will pornography end?' the reader asked.
*'If we **cannot** change, with the end of humankind,' came my reply.*